"Uh, this might sound strange, but who is Piper? And why is she in the emergency room?"

Kassia turned toward him. Her mouth dropped open. "You mean she didn't tell you tonight, either? She hasn't said anything after all this time?"

Kassia's remarks made Theo even more uneasy. Why would Lexie feel the need to hide someone from him? "Uh, no."

"Sorry. I just thought Lexie would have told you at dinner tonight." Kassia pointed to the couch. "You'd better sit down."

Theo felt a knot form in his throat. At the moment his feet didn't feel like moving. "I'll stand—thanks."

"I'll be glad to sit." Kassia dropped onto the couch, then looked up at Theo. "I can't believe she didn't say anything. Maybe I shouldn't, either." Kassia stared at her feet.

"You might as well tell me. I'm going to find out sooner or later." He glanced toward the kitchen. "From the looks of things Lexie is in no condition to tell me herself."

Kassia nodded. "All right then. I'll tell you." She took in a deep breath but kept her gaze on her feet. "Piper is Lexie's little girl."

TAMELA HANCOCK MURRAY shares her home in Virginia with her godly husband and their two beautiful daughters. The car is her second home as she chauffeurs her girls to their many activities related to church, school, cheerleading, and music. She is thankful that several local Christian radio stations allow her family to spend much of their driving time in praise and worship. Tamela hopes that her stories of God-centered romance edify and entertain her sisters in Christ. You may e-mail Tamela at: Write_to_Tamela@juno.com

Books by Tamela Hancock Murray

HEARTSONG PRESENTS
HP213—Picture of Love
HP408—Destinations
HP453—The Elusive Mr. Perfect
HP501—Thrill of the Hunt
HP544—A Light Among Shadows
HP568—Loveswept

Don't miss out on any of our super romances. Write to us at the following address for information on our newest releases and club information.

Heartsong Presents Readers' Service
PO Box 719
Uhrichsville, OH 44683

Or check out our Web site at www.heartsongpresents.com

More Than Friends

Tamela Hancock Murray

Heartsong Presents

A Note from the Author:
I love to hear from my readers! You may correspond with me by writing:

Tamela Hancock Murray
Author Relations
PO Box 719
Uhrichsville, OH 44683

ISBN 1-59310-098-1

MORE THAN FRIENDS

Our mission is to publish and distribute inspirational products offering exceptional value and biblical encouragement to the masses.

prologue

"Mommy, don't go!" Tears spilled from four-year-old Piper's brown eyes.

"I wish I didn't have to, Honey." Lexie Zoltan bent down and hugged her daughter.

As Piper's face burrowed into her shoulder, Lexie gazed beyond the columns of her childhood home and noted the irony of the idyllic day. A cloudless blue sky and light breeze carried with it the scent of freshly mown grass. Any other time she would have relished the chance to relax on the porch swing. She could imagine herself sipping a glass of iced tea flavored with a sprig of fresh mint, watching Piper jump rope and run around the expansive yard where she once played as a little girl. But not today. She had never felt worse—except on the day Curt died.

Squeezing Piper, Lexie struggled to keep from shedding her own tears, but to no avail. A tear hit the corner of her mouth, leaving a salty taste. Burying her face in Piper's hair, the same blond as Curt's, Lexie refused to worry about whether her dark mascara and pink blush would rub off on her daughter's hair.

"Why do you have to go, Mommy? Can't I go with you?" Piper uttered between sniffles.

Lexie held on to her daughter, her face pressing against Piper's T-shirt. She didn't dare look at Piper, lest her heart shatter beyond repair. "Not this time," she murmured.

"When can I come with you?"

"Soon. I promise." Lexie forced herself to break the embrace. She took Piper's soft little chin in her hand and met her trusting but inquisitive eyes. She swallowed. How could she leave her preschooler? Would she still see the same trust in those eyes when she returned?

Heavenly Father, keep us in Your tender loving care while we are apart.

"When?" Piper persisted. "Tomorrow?" Hope lit up her face.

Lexie shook her head. "I'm afraid it will be longer than that. I have to get settled in Richmond."

"But I want to come with you. I want to live in our house there."

"I know. But we don't have a house there, at least not yet," Lexie explained. "I'll be staying with Miss Kassia. You remember her, don't you? My friend from school?"

Piper shook her head.

Lexie stroked Piper's head. Of course the child wouldn't remember Kassia. "As soon as I find us a nice place to live, I'll come back for you. It won't take long."

The bang of the screen door turned Lexie's attention to her parents. Mom and Dad had given Lexie a few moments to say good-bye to Piper. Their entrance signaled the time to leave had come—too soon.

Her mother's lips formed a tight line, and her eyes held a look of sadness. Her father's arms were folded tightly across his chest, resting over his ample stomach. Lexie knew both parents felt ambivalent about her decision to start a new life in another state, but she had to leave North Carolina, her childhood home, with its problems—and its memories.

They didn't understand, but they supported her by promising to care for Piper for a short time. Maybe they never would understand why she had to move or why this step toward newfound independence was so important to her. She had to succeed. She just had to.

She turned back to Piper. "Just think of all the fun you'll have with Grammy and Pops while I'm away."

Piper barely smiled. "I know."

"I'll be back as soon as I can." Lexie gave her daughter one last squeeze. Tears filled her eyes when she had to let her go.

"You can still change your mind. You'll always have a home here with us," her father reassured her.

The urge to take him up on his offer was almost too much to resist. Lexie glanced at the window of her room, unchanged since her teen years. That room would always represent warmth, security, and comfort—feelings she didn't want to relinquish. But what she needed to accomplish took precedence.

She drew in a breath and squared her shoulders. "I know. But I have to try."

"I guess this is good-bye then," her mother said.

"Oh, Mom. I'm not going so far away. Only a few hours."

"That's too far for me, but you have to do what you have to do."

"Drive defensively," Dad cautioned.

"Okay, now I can leave." Lexie winked at her father and hugged him.

"If your dad didn't tell you to drive defensively, you'd think something was wrong, wouldn't you?" her mother said as she embraced Lexie.

Then Lexie bent over and gave Piper one last hug and kiss. "Be good now."

"I will."

Lexie slid behind the wheel of her modest decade-old car and pulled out of her parents' driveway. Unable to resist one last look, she waved and blew kisses to her little girl. Piper sent kisses back and waved with both arms in return. Her parents and daughter stood in front of the brick rambler. White shutters framed the windows, and their old calico cat was slinking away from its hiding place behind a boxwood shrub. She put the car in drive and pressed on the gas pedal.

At the end of the dirt road, the right-hand turn she took seemed to signal a departure from everything she had ever known and loved. She had driven this country road a thousand times. She knew each dip and bend. The interstate, with its open space and unspoken promises, would soon stretch before her.

She took a tissue from the box on the seat beside her and wiped away the last of her tears. "This is it. No more crying. I'm on my way. It's now or never. With God's help, I will succeed."

one

Lexie set her suitcases down on the bed in the small second bedroom Kassia showed her in the rear of the apartment. Several pictures that weren't to her taste adorned beige walls, and she could tell the dresser was too small to hold the clothes she usually kept folded at home. Still, Kassia was being generous to let her share the apartment for less than half the rent until she could find a place where she could afford to live on her own. Far be it for Lexie to complain.

"Thanks for the room." Lexie hoped her repeated expressions of gratitude would spur Kassia to leave her so she could unpack in privacy.

Kassia didn't budge. "I hope you brought some good clothes."

Lexie shrugged and opened the smaller of her two suitcases. "Just clothes for work. No evening gowns or anything. Why? Did you enter me in the Miss America pageant?"

"If I did, you'd win. But I have a good consolation prize." She paused. "Theo Powers."

Lexie's stomach seemed to jump into her throat. "Theo. Oh. Well, that's nice of him to think of me. I guess he has a wife by now. I'm sure she's pretty, too."

Kassia shook her head. "I have good news for you. He's not married."

So Theo had stayed single. An image of his striking face and toned physique flashed into her mind. "I don't believe it."

"He's probably been waiting for you all these years." Kassia sat on the foot of Lexie's bed. "I think he's still holding a torch for you, Lexie."

"Don't be ridiculous. I wouldn't flatter myself to think such a thing." A warm feeling rushed over her, though, just imagining he still cared in the least.

"You'll think differently once you see him again. I know he wants to see you."

"You told him I was moving back to town?"

"Of course. I remember how tight the two of you were back in school."

Lexie remembered, too. She and Theo had been inseparable until Curt entered the picture. Feeling abandoned, Theo hadn't taken well to her marriage. But Lexie had her reasons. And she didn't need new problems now. "I wish you hadn't said anything, Kassia."

"This town may look big, but it really isn't. Whether I said anything or not, you'd run into him sooner or later."

"Later would have been better. Or not at all." She busied herself transferring blue jeans, T-shirts, blouses, and church dresses from the suitcase to hangers, hoping they would fit in the small closet. Lexie refused to let her gaze meet her roommate's.

"Why won't you even consider it?"

Why not? She and Theo had once been close, but there was a deal breaker. He'd always said he never wanted children.

Lexie had been away from her daughter for only a few hours, and she already missed her. She yearned to touch Piper's face. . .but instead returned to unpacking.

"I didn't come back to Richmond after all this time to find a husband," Lexie said. "I came here because of my job promotion."

A promotion I pray will help me clear my debts. A job in another state, away from the painful memories. And the guilt. Curt died, and it's all my fault. Maybe if I can make a go of it here, away from the town where he died, I can forgive myself.

"Besides," Lexie added, "it was high time for me to grow up."

Kassia shrugged. "I guess we all come to that place in our lives. Or at least we should."

"Once I get settled in my own place," Lexie continued, "I'll send for Piper and get out of your hair."

"You're not in my hair. I'm glad for the company." The brunette's smile conveyed genuine emotion.

Lexie gave her old college roommate a hug. "Thanks, Kassia. I really do appreciate you."

"You know you can always count on me." Kassia returned her light squeeze. "I love having you as a roommate again. It'll be like old times."

"You mean pizza and popcorn at midnight? Studying for midterms and finals?" Lexie scrunched her nose. "I'll take the pizza, but skip the tests—thank you very much. And I definitely wouldn't want to go through Dr. Stein's macroeconomics class again."

"But wasn't all the trouble worth it, to graduate with an economics degree? Try hitting the job market with liberal arts and a minor in Renaissance history."

"You're doing great! What are you complaining about?"

"Only because my uncle found a place for me in his office. Look at Morgan," Kassia said, referring to another classmate. "She was laid off from her job three months ago and still hasn't found anything else."

"As if she has to worry. It's not like Gary doesn't have a good job." Lexie regretted the tinge of envy in her voice. She and Curt had never enjoyed job security.

"I guess. But I think she's worried since they just moved into their new house." Kassia grinned. "You know, Theo has a good consulting job and a nice place on a cul-de-sac. I've seen it. That house is bigger than Morgan's. All new, with spotless beige carpets and everything painted off-white."

"Sounds inspired."

"Oh, it is." A laugh escaped Kassia's lips. "He managed to

get some shades on the windows, but that's about it. There's stuff from college thrown around as if he just moved in yesterday. I don't think he's bought a stick of furniture in ten years. Believe me, Theo's place is ready for a woman's touch."

"Good for him. I hope he finds the right woman to decorate it in grand style. Maybe someone like you," she teased.

"Me?" Kassia chuckled. "Theo's a great guy, but we couldn't ignite enough sparks between us to start a fire with a box of kitchen matches and the biggest pile of dry brush in the world." She pointed a finger at Lexie. "But the two of you could rub two sticks together in a torrential downpour and start a bonfire."

Lexie turned away from Kassia and occupied herself by folding several pairs of socks. Unbidden, a picture of Theo flitted across her mind. Brown hair, streaked from summers as a lifeguard, accentuated tanned skin, and eyes the color of melted semisweet chocolate. All those looks and a brain, too. "That was a long time ago," she forced herself to admit.

"He had a lot of promise back then, and as far as I can see he's lived up to his potential."

"You do realize I'd never pursue a man because of his job, don't you?" Lexie knew her voice sounded artificially bright.

"I have to agree 'gold-digger' doesn't describe you, Lexie. Besides, I can't imagine you as anything but independent. Even as Curt's wife you kept your own identity." Kassia stopped herself. Her face flushed pink.

"It's okay. You don't have to act as if it's taboo to mention his name." She stopped folding her socks and looked at Kassia.

"Yeah. But I know you're still hurting."

Kassia spoke the truth. How could Lexie not be hurting? Curt's accident on the construction site would always be with her. He'd gone home to the Lord much too soon. Lexie never quit blaming herself for his death. If only she hadn't been so greedy, he would still be alive today. "I always will hurt."

"Maybe seeing Theo will make you feel better."

"Feel better? No way." Lexie resumed folding with more vengeance than necessary. "I can't see anyone else. I can't do that to Curt."

"It's been two years," Kassia pointed out. "No one will think you're being unfaithful to Curt after all this time."

Lexie looked directly into Kassia's eyes. "No, Kassia. I won't see Theo. And that's final."

❧

Theo Powers swallowed the lump in his throat as he walked toward the two-story, red-brick apartment building. He hadn't remembered being this nervous in a long while.

Looking for a distraction, he noted the care professional landscapers had taken to keep the grounds pristine. Some garden spots were filled with strategically planted bushes—some with red leaves, others with green—and bordered by blue-faced pansies. Each plant looked robust and in full flower, evidence that any wilted specimen was yanked and replaced without hesitation to keep a uniform appearance at the upscale complex. Along sidewalks and the edge of the common areas were what looked like every type of flowering plant known to thrive in Virginia. Pink and white dogwood trees, apple trees, Asian pear trees, azaleas, and other flowers burst with color. They made a beautiful picture. He could only imagine their lovely scent. Too bad his stuffy nose prohibited him from taking in the sweet fragrance.

Observing the blooms, Theo wondered how anyone could doubt God's existence and His intelligent design. He had only one question. Why did the Creator choose to afflict him with allergies to pollen?

He sneezed.

Theo paused on the sidewalk. At that moment a group of young men in a 1970s muscle car sped past. The drumbeat and wail of guitars from rock music pulsated from open windows. In such a presence he felt wimpy extracting one of the ever present white tissues from his pocket. As Theo sneezed into it twice more, he imagined the young men inside the car were laughing at him. When he ventured a look, he saw them staring back but not laughing. Those workouts had paid off.

He sneezed once more. Why didn't the pills the doctor prescribed work or, at least, work better? For the thousandth time he considered allergy shots.

Naturally he and Lexie were reuniting on a day when his allergies were at their worst. How could she enjoy being with someone who was constantly sneezing and coughing and watery-eyed? Then again, if he delayed their meeting until his symptoms subsided, they'd likely not see each other until months from now. He didn't want to wait.

Theo stuffed the tissue back into the pocket of his chino pants and tightened the grip on the dozen red roses he had picked up for Lexie at the grocery store. At least he didn't sneeze around roses. Not that he'd had much contact with roses lately. He hadn't bought flowers for a woman in years.

Theo groaned before straightening himself to his full height of just over six feet. He put on the confident expression he always wore when he felt jittery and climbed the two flights of stairs to Kassia's apartment.

Kassia had called a week ago to let Theo know that Lexie planned to move back to town, and long suppressed feelings had emerged. He'd missed Lexie and the easy friendship they once shared. When she'd moved back to North Carolina after graduation, disappointment had flooded him. The feelings were compounded when, a few months later, he watched her walk down the aisle of a little country church, dressed in flowing white, to marry Curt.

He preferred to think of a more distant time, when Lexie was a carefree coed. Burnished gold hair flowed almost down to her slender waist. Eyes as luminous as sapphires sparkled with ready laughter. Lexie had been pretty and popular in school. So popular that Theo hadn't been alarmed when Curt Zoltan, a jock known more for brawn than brains, joined their study group to cram for a history exam. Before he knew what had happened, study sessions turned to romance for Lexie and Curt. If only Theo hadn't taken her for granted. If only he hadn't misinterpreted Curt's attention toward Lexie. If only he'd spoken up in time to let Lexie know his true feelings—that he wanted to be more than friends. If he had, perhaps Curt wouldn't have stolen her away.

Theo delayed his steps as he walked down the hall, in keeping with his resolution to take things slowly with Lexie. Kassia had told him Curt had died tragically in a construction accident. From what little he'd heard over the years, Theo gathered that Curt had been an ideal Christian husband. Theo sighed. Who wanted to compete with a ghost?

I probably don't stand a chance after all these years. But I have to see her. I have to try. There's no other way I can get her out of my mind.

He stopped in front of Kassia's apartment. His heart beating rapidly, Theo fought the temptation to call her on his cell phone and tell her he wouldn't be visiting after all. He stood there a moment and adjusted the bouquet in his left hand.

The door opened. Too late. The decision had been made.

two

"Hi, Theo." Kassia's broad smile covered her face, an expression he didn't see on her often. She stood in the doorway and twisted a dark curl around her finger.

"Hi." Theo had hoped Lexie would answer the door.

"Nice roses."

He looked at them. "I thought so." He felt awkward standing in the hallway. "Uh, aren't you going to invite me in?"

"Oh. Yeah. Sure." Kassia lurched as though she had just been awakened from a deep sleep. She stepped aside. "Come on in."

"She's here, isn't she?" he said in a low voice.

Kassia nodded. "She got here a couple of hours ago," she answered in a stage whisper. "She's hardly had time to settle in yet."

Just then Lexie called from the next room. "Who's that, Kassia?"

Lexie! He'd forgotten the sweetness of her voice. Without warning, emotions he thought he would never again experience rose to the surface.

"Is it the delivery man?" Light footfalls approached the living area, bringing the sound of her voice closer. "I'm still expecting a few things—" In an instant she stood at the entrance to the kitchen. The woman he loved! He took in a breath. Theo knew his love for her had never died.

As soon as her blue gaze met Theo's stare, she stopped.

"Lexie!" The voice coming out of his mouth sounded eager. Too eager.

He fought the impulse to run toward her. His hand, still

holding the roses, jerked in an awkward motion. First he held them out toward her, then pressed them back against his chest. Their freshman psychology professor would have said the gesture reflected Theo's inner debate.

"Theo." Instead of the look of pleasure he longed to see, Lexie's face revealed a combination of surprise, discomfort and—could it be—fear?

"Hello." Theo snapped out of his dream state. His second greeting sounded much more restrained than his initial outburst. He swooshed the flowers behind his back.

Lexie turned her attention to Kassia. "What is he doing here?" Her tone seemed almost accusatory.

A sheepish expression covered Kassia's face. "I, uh, I invited him."

"As soon as Kassia told me you'd be coming in today, I decided I'd like to take you both out to dinner. Sort of like a 'welcome home' celebration," Theo added.

"You did?" Kassia asked. "Oh, how nice of you, Theo." She turned to Lexie. "Isn't that nice of Theo?"

He wished he hadn't let his emotions carry him away, but he tried to make the best of the situation. "I thought we could go to that seafood place on Cary Street where we always wanted to eat but could never afford. Remember that?"

"Oh, I remember." A nervous titter sprang from Kassia's lips.

Theo took a moment to drink in Lexie's appearance. He wouldn't have thought it possible, but she looked even more beautiful now than she had in college. Her hair had grown a few shades darker, just enough to accentuate her creamy skin. Her hair no longer fell to her waist, a fact he noted with regret. Instead she wore it in a shoulder length flip that somehow managed to look retro and up to date at once. The style became her, he realized. Framing her face, it drew more attention to her blue eyes and pert nose. The bone structure of her heart shaped face looked more prominent than before, but the soft sleeveless turtleneck and blue jeans she wore revealed she hadn't lost so much weight as to appear gaunt. In fact, she epitomized perfection. Just perfect. But then maybe she always had been.

"I'll even treat you both to the most expensive dinner on the menu. Won't it be great, after all this time? We won't have to pinch pennies or argue over how to split the bill," Theo said.

"I don't know if I have to eat the most expensive thing on the menu, but I sure could go for some surf and turf," Kassia said. "How about you, Lexie?"

Instead of brightening into an anticipated smile, Lexie's face darkened, and her mouth set itself in a thin line. "Thanks for thinking of me, but I really can't go."

Why not? Theo waited for her to offer a valid excuse, but instead she folded her hands across her chest, raising a silent but visible barrier.

"That's the first time I've known you to turn down a free dinner," Theo joked.

His jesting did nothing to lighten Lexie's countenance or mood.

"That's just it, Theo. You don't know me anymore." He didn't like her edgy tone.

"That doesn't mean—"

Her face and expression softened with apology. "I'm sorry, but I can't go with you to dinner. Thanks for the offer." She tilted her head toward her roommate. "Why don't you go ahead with Kassia and have a nice time?" Before Theo could protest, Lexie retreated into the bedroom and shut the door behind her with a thud.

"What's the matter with her?" Theo asked.

"I don't know. I have no idea why she's acting like this. Maybe she's just tired." Kassia shook her head so hard her curls moved back and forth.

"Or maybe I moved too fast," Theo wondered aloud. "Maybe I should have waited for her to settle in before trying to meet again. Or inviting her anyplace." He brightened at a thought. "Should I try again in a couple of days? Maybe this coming Saturday?"

Kassia shook her head. "I'm not so sure even that would help."

Theo dropped his arm to his side, leaving the roses facing the floor. They looked as dejected as he felt. "Oh."

"Look—it's not you," Kassia explained. "It's Lexie. For some reason she has this idea she can't see you because of Curt. As if she's being unfaithful or something."

"Unfaithful? That's ridiculous."

"I think so, too. I'd hoped that seeing you would change her mind."

"Maybe she's disappointed with how I've changed since she last saw me."

Kassia looked him up and down in an exaggerated manner. "I don't think so."

Theo grinned. He and Kassia had been friends too long for them to entertain any romantic notions toward each other. "Thanks for the boost. I needed that."

"You're welcome." She sighed. "Maybe I overreacted when I told you not to try later. Why don't you? She's been through a lot. I'm sure she'll be in a better frame of mind once she settles in."

"Yeah." Theo had his doubts. He handed Kassia the roses. "Here. Why don't you enjoy these at least? There's no point in letting them go to waste."

"They're beautiful. I wish they really were for me." Kassia sniffed one of the blooms. "These just might be your ticket."

"Really? If she turns down a free dinner that easily, she must be a pretty hard nut to crack these days."

"You'd be surprised how far a few roses can take you, even

with independent, modern women." Kassia disappeared into the kitchen with the flowers.

In her absence he studied the familiar living room. Kassia hadn't acquired much in the way of décor since school days. She had upgraded the old nineteen-inch television set that had been in her dorm room to a larger screen, and the computer looked new. Other than that she had the same furniture, a mixture of castoffs and cheap bookshelves he had helped her cart in when she first rented the place after graduation. The sameness offered a bit of comfortable familiarity in an ever changing world.

"Are you still up for that surf and turf?" Theo called.

Kassia reappeared with the roses, which she had placed in a cut-glass vase with water. "You don't have to do that. You came to see Lexie, not me." She held the roses toward him. "Don't these look even more beautiful arranged in the vase?" She smiled and set them on the end table beside the sofa.

"Yes, if I do say so myself. And just to compliment you on your fine talent as a florist, I'll take you to dinner as I promised."

She looked toward the kitchen. "Well, I hadn't made any other dinner plans, so a good meal out sounds like a plan. Are you sure?"

"Sure, I'm sure. Hey, I'm not as nice as you'd like to think. I have a motive," he confessed. "I have to eat, too."

Kassia laughed. "You convinced me. Surf and turf it is."

≈

Loneliness wrapped itself around Lexie when she heard the door shut behind Theo and Kassia. She had overheard enough of their conversation to realize they had gone to the restaurant without her.

Why did she have to be so stubborn and turn down a perfectly good meal and let Kassia go out alone with Theo? And why did a feeling of discomfort tug at the pit of her stomach?

She'd told them to go without her. They had every right to take her up on her suggestion.

She grimaced. Who cared about the meal? She'd missed Theo's company—or lack thereof. Seeing him again brought forth unexpected feelings—feelings she had long forgotten. She wished she hadn't passed up the chance to spend time with him again, to renew their friendship, or maybe—

She shook such unwelcome thoughts out of her head.

Well, fine. If they wanted to go out and have a good time together and leave her alone, fine. Fine with her. She felt in no mood to put on a good face and engage in idle chitchat in a public place. Not tonight.

She made her way into the small kitchen and inspected Kassia's refrigerator. Only a half head of lettuce, a few carrots, and a carton of skim milk occupied the shelves. Maybe she should have gone out for seafood after all.

She opened the freezer and counted six frozen burritos. Bingo! She popped an extra spicy beef and bean burrito in the microwave. While she waited, Lexie stared at the apartment door.

Inviting Theo to visit on the first day she arrived in town? How could she forgive Kassia for ambushing her like that?

Better yet, how could she forgive herself for her silent reaction to seeing him again? Her heart betrayed her with its rapid beating and its sudden yearning.

The years had barely touched Theo. Sun streaks from summers as a lifeguard had given way to a natural brown. She realized she liked the way Theo's hair looked with his eyes, the color of fine mahogany. And from the way his orange polo shirt draped across his chest, Theo hadn't missed too many days at the gym. If only—

The phone rang. Lexie rushed to answer, hoping it was Piper. "Hello?"

"Mommy?" The voice removed all doubts about her decision

to stay home instead of going out with Kassia and Theo.

"Piper!" Lexie smiled into the phone. "Yes, Honey, it's me! Have you had a good day with Grammy and Pops?"

"Yep!" Piper began a long story about her day with her grandparents. Apparently she had made friends with the other little girls in the park and had seen someone from Sunday school.

"Did you play on the swings?"

"Yeah! Grammy doesn't push me as high as you do, though."

Lexie imagined her little girl, blond hair flying in the breeze, begging her grandma to push her higher. "I know you had a good time all the same."

"Yeah! Grammy let me have money for the gum machine. I got a bracelet."

"That sounds like fun. I miss you. Do you miss me?"

She hesitated. "A little bit."

"I miss you a lot bit." Lexie chuckled. "I know you're having fun with Grammy and Pops. I don't get to have fun the way you do."

"When are you coming home, Mommy?"

"Soon." Her heart lurched. They would be together in a matter of weeks. The time could not pass quickly enough for Lexie.

"Grammy wants to talk," Piper said. "I'm gonna hand her the phone now. Don't hang up, okay?"

"All right, Honey. I love you! Here's a big smooch." Lexie made a kissing sound into the phone.

"I love you, too, Mommy." Piper smacked her lips back. "Here's Grammy."

She assured her mother that everything in her life was humming along at a smooth pace, then hung up a few moments later. She remained fixed in the chair. Piper's feelings came first.

Then why did Lexie feel so confused?

three

The next afternoon Lexie was humming the chorus of a melody as she sorted laundry in her room.

"I'm home," Kassia called.

Lexie heard the door shut behind her friend. "I'm in here," she responded, knowing Kassia could follow her voice in the small apartment. "I'm doing a load of reds so a dress I want to wear to work will be clean. I'll be glad to throw in anything of yours. Well, except maybe whites. Unless you want them to turn out pink."

"Cute," Kassia replied from the hallway. "I'll look and see." Moments later, she entered Lexie's room, a few red items in her hand. She threw them in the small pile. "Thanks." She smiled. "You seem to be in a better mood today."

"You said it." Lexie threw a scratchy red broadcloth blouse in the pile of red, orange, and magenta clothing.

"So you're not mad at me?"

"Mad at you? What for?"

"You know what for. For going without you last night. I would have apologized to you after I got home, but you were already asleep."

"I went to bed early." Lexie turned to Kassia. "I admit I was a little annoyed, but then I realized I have no right to be mad. You and Theo invited me to dinner. I was the one who wouldn't go."

"You may as well have been there," Kassia said. "Theo couldn't stop talking about you all night."

"He couldn't?" The unsettling emotions she had felt the previous night returned.

23

"No. I could tell that seeing you again had an effect on him."

"Really?" Lexie blurted out. "He's not hoping for—?" How could she express herself without sounding like a total egomaniac?

"You mean," Kassia asked, smiling, "he's not hoping for a romance?"

Her face flushed hot. "Or anything else, I guess."

"I don't know," Kassia answered. "But I think he was pretty disappointed you didn't go out with us. You know, it wouldn't have hurt to give him a chance."

"I might seem harsh to you, but there are things you don't know."

"Like what?"

Lexie felt no desire to elaborate. Besides, if she argued with her friend, Kassia would defend Theo. Then she would insist that Lexie spend time with him. She refused to consider any relationships based on guilt. She harbored enough remorse over her husband's death to last a thousand lifetimes.

"Well?"

"Let's just say it's a good thing I didn't go," Lexie said. "Mom and Dad called while you were gone. I got to talk to Piper."

"I know you wouldn't have missed that for the world." Kassia smiled. "She's probably having a great time being spoiled by her grandparents."

"You're not kidding." Reviewing the hamper's contents, Lexie decided her orange capri pants were bright enough not to be affected by the dyes in the rest of the load. She scooped them out of the ivory-colored wicker container.

"Are you sure about those pants?"

Lexie studied them, then nodded. "I've washed them a couple of times. And I'll be using cold water."

"Decisions, decisions." Kassia chuckled. "Not quite as glamorous as our real jobs, huh?"

"I don't know if you'd call my job glamorous, but it's the best one I've ever had. Ms. Smith has given me an interesting project. Plus she doesn't breathe down my neck all day. I really enjoy the work."

"That must be novel for a technical writer," Kassia observed. The corners of her mouth turned up.

"Very cute," Lexie noted. "I know technical writing seems dry, especially for people who'd rather read novels."

"Like me." Kassia raised her hand.

"I know." Lexie grinned. "But you'd be surprised at how rewarding my job can be."

"Oh, sure." Kassia glanced upward. "So many instruction manuals, so little time. How many creative ways can you say, 'Press the red button'?"

"Technical writing actually is very creative," Lexie said. "I look at it as helping people understand what they've just bought. If it weren't for people like me, owner's manuals would be written by design engineers, heavy on the technical jargon. If people who buy our products read the manual I write and follow the directions, they'll be getting the most out of whatever they buy since I work the technical terms into everyday phrases."

"Assuming anyone actually reads the manual." Kassia shook her head. "I hate to tell you this, but very few people get as excited about instruction manuals as you do."

Lexie scrunched her nose. "I know. Well, if they don't read the directions, then it's their own fault if they don't understand how to use what they buy. And if they don't learn, they're not being the best stewards they can of the money the Lord gives them."

Kassia let out an exaggerated sigh. "You haven't changed a bit, Lexie. Everything's a sermon with you, isn't it? I don't see why you don't go to seminary."

Lexie tossed a red-and-black patterned blouse onto a pile

of similar colors. "No, thanks. Teaching Sunday school is challenging enough for me."

"Doesn't sound half as exciting as what I have planned for this evening." Kassia cocked her head to one side and looked at Lexie from the corners of her eyes.

Lexie made a mental list of Kassia's favorite ways to spend a night out. "Let me guess. You're going to use the gift certificate your mom gave you for your birthday and splurge on a massage."

"That sounds heavenly." Kassia closed her eyes and let out a deep sigh.

"May I join you?"

"Yes and no."

"Huh?"

"Yes, you can join me, but, no, it's not for a massage."

Lexie couldn't hide her curiosity. "What then?"

"I have a date."

"A real date, eh? Not just a get-together with the women at work?"

"Nope." She tilted her head. "I"—she placed a forefinger on her chest—"have a real date. Dinner out with a man."

"Great!" Lexie said with genuine happiness. "Then what do you want me along for? I doubt you want a chaperone. Besides, I believe in 'two's company, but three's a crowd.'"

"But four works out pretty well."

"Four!" Lexie groaned and placed her hands on her hips. "No, not again. You just tried to set me up last night. Don't tell me you were on the phone all day at work, making plans for tonight, too."

"No way. My job's too important to me. I allow very little time for social planning," Kassia assured her. "It's just that Brad called and, well. . ." She hesitated.

"Brad? The one you told me about, the one who works down the hall from you?" Lexie's voice rose with excitement.

Kassia nodded. "The same one."

"Good for you. I know you've had your eye on him for some time. And that's exactly why I shouldn't barge in." Lexie wagged her forefinger at Kassia. "I don't want to ruin things for you."

"You won't," Kassia assured her.

Lexie shook her head. "Just call whoever my date is and tell him it's off."

"I can't do that. It's already planned. Just consider the free dinner a payback for my running out on you last night."

"You didn't run out on me." Lexie felt tempted, though. Seeing Theo again had stirred her heartstrings in a way she liked. And didn't like. Reigniting a long lost relationship held no appeal for her, especially with Theo. He had always been adamant about never wanting children. How could he accept Piper?

"Okay," Kassia said. "Maybe Theo and I didn't exactly run out on you. But I'd like to show you a good time while we're roomies all the same. You won't have the freedom to come and go as you please once Piper gets here, you know."

"But I don't want freedom. At least, not complete freedom as you have. If I did, I'd just leave Piper with Mom and Dad indefinitely."

Kassia placed a sympathetic hand on Lexie's shoulder. "Lexie, if I could have picked any mom but my own, I would have picked you. You have to be one of the most unselfish women I know. But you're a woman, too. Need I remind you that you're still in your twenties? You're not an old lady. I think you forget that sometimes."

Lexie swallowed. How could she argue? "You're not setting me up with Jake, are you?"

"Jake? No way. Even I can't stand listening to him brag. Nope, it's someone you'll like very much."

"Well. . ." Doubts tugged at her. "I know you have the best

of intentions, and I love you to death for it; but I've already told you I did not come here to find a husband. I just want to get established in a great job and settled so Piper can have a good life. The kind of life she deserves."

"And she will. But you owe it to yourself to be happy, too, don't you?"

Lexie twitched her mouth into a playful grin. "What are you selling—cars, soda, or hair color?"

Kassia laughed. "I'm selling life. A good life. One you can't buy. Come on, Lexie. If you don't go for the guy, at least look at it as a free meal."

Lexie folded her arms. "Isn't that kind of mercenary?"

"Only if you let yourself think of it that way," Kassia added. "Okay, I'll make a deal with you. If you really don't like the guy, you can pay for your own dinner. Or you can pay for your own dinner, anyway. How's that?"

Lexie weighed Kassia's suggestion. "I appreciate the offer, but I honestly don't want to go. I was planning to stay in tonight." She tilted her head toward the mound of dirty clothing on the floor. "Wouldn't you say I have a few things to do? Besides, I have a good book I've been saving for this occasion." To prove her point, she grabbed her book from the night table and held it up for Kassia to see.

"*How to Be a Success in Twenty-One Days?*" Kassia's eyes widened. "Don't you think you're already a success?"

Lexie shrugged. "Good advice is worth reading."

"Good advice or not, success can wait until tomorrow night." Kassia viewed the laundry. "On second thought I think I'll take this out." She retrieved a skirt with red flowers on a white background.

"That's probably a good idea. Maybe you should wash it by hand."

Kassia grimaced. "Maybe I'll just take it in to the dry cleaners."

"I know!" Lexie exclaimed. "I can do that for you instead of going out."

"You're not getting out of this dinner that easily." Kassia's voice took on a pleading tone. "You really have to go with me."

"I do?" Lexie looked at her friend suspiciously.

"Yeah." Kassia paused. "I sort of, uh, promised you'd be there."

"Kassia!" Lexie moaned. "Oh, all right. But don't tie up any more evenings for me without asking, okay? I can take care of my own social calendar."

Kassia rewarded Lexie with a big smile. If spending an evening out meant that much to her, she would make the sacrifice. Lexie relied on Kassia's friendship. Without her generous offer to share the apartment until she could gain financial security, she'd be living in lesser accommodations with a stranger. Lexie knew she owed Kassia a lot.

She looked down at her faded blue T-shirt and gray gym shorts. "I'd better put on something that's a little nicer than this. How much time do I have?"

Kassia glanced at her watch. "It's already a quarter to six. You have exactly one hour. Think you can make yourself look good enough for Le Bistro in that amount of time?"

"Le Bistro?" She recalled reading a review that had raved over the restaurant's high priced entrees. "I'll be sure to bring my credit card."

"Trust me—you won't be paying for dinner," Kassia assured her. "You'll like this guy, remember?"

Lexie shrugged. "So you say."

Almost an hour later, Lexie emerged from her room looking like a different woman. She had freshened her hair with hot rollers. Touches of light color on her eyes and face brought out her natural beauty without calling attention to the fact that she wore makeup.

She had chosen an Irish linen shift for the occasion. Its

fresh peach color complimented her complexion. A few extra minutes spent applying peach polish to her nails paid off in colorful dividends. A gold necklace, earrings, and bracelet in a matching set went well with sandals decorated with gold accents and low heels.

When Kassia saw her roommate, she let out a whistle. "I thought you were prepared not to like your date."

"I'm not dressing for him. I'm dressing for myself." She looked directly at Kassia as she spoke.

As a young widow caring for a daughter and holding a job that didn't require a suit, Lexie found few opportunities to dress the way she liked to as a woman. She felt no qualms about her dress. The linen shift had been bought for church, not to attract a man.

The apostle Peter's words from his first epistle passed through her mind: *"Your beauty should not come from outward adornment, such as braided hair and the wearing of gold jewelry and fine clothes. Instead, it should be that of your inner self, the unfading beauty of a gentle and quiet spirit, which is of great worth in God's sight."*

Kassia's teasing brought her back to the present. "You're dressing for yourself, huh? Who are you trying to kid?" She surveyed Lexie's appearance. "Looks to me like you've been saving that dress in your closet in hopes of snagging a guy."

"No, I haven't." Realizing she sounded testy, Lexie softened her tone. "At least, I didn't think I was." Lexie glanced at her outfit. "Is it really that daring?"

"Not daring. Just flattering." Kassia winked. "He'll like it."

Lexie raised her hands in frustration. "Forget it. I'm changing." She turned back toward the hall.

"Wait!" Kassia called. "I was just joking. Besides, we don't have time. We have to leave right now."

"Aren't they coming to pick us up?" Lexie asked.

"No. We're meeting them there."

Lexie ran her hands over the shift. "It won't take me a minute to put on something else."

"You'd better not! Trust me—you look fine."

Lexie took note of Kassia's dress. A skimpy black number with spaghetti straps and v-neck, its short length complimented Kassia's thin legs that seemed to melt into strappy sandals with high heels. By comparison Lexie did seem to be playing the part of a school marm.

"All right. I'll take your word for it," she conceded. "Let's go."

The ride in Kassia's small car passed all too quickly. Lexie's hands felt clammy, and her foot tapped to an unheard tune on the floorboard. She wished they could ride around all night so she wouldn't have to meet Mr. Mystery Man. Unless—

No. Kassia wouldn't do that. She wouldn't think of asking Theo to be her date. Not after last night. Lexie hoped her date would be someone new. Someone she didn't know. Someone who didn't remember her the way she once was, before her life fell apart.

She didn't want to face Theo. Not after the way she treated him, when really he was only trying to show her a little hospitality as a welcome back gesture. How could she ever make it up to him for being so rude?

Maybe she could call him sometime. Sure, that was it. Times had changed. Lexie wasn't her grandmother. She didn't have to wait by the telephone, hoping against hope a man would call. Then again, if she called, Theo might misread her gesture as a ploy for romantic attention. And she couldn't have that.

"Here we are." Kassia pulled the car into an underground parking lot and handed the attendant a few dollars to cover the flat fee for the evening's parking privileges.

Lexie reached for her purse. "Here. Let me help with that."

Kassia eschewed the offer with a wave of her hand, then pressed the gas pedal. "You can cover us next time."

At one time Lexie would have objected, but money was too

tight for her to display the generosity she felt in her heart.

"Are you excited?" Kassia whispered a few moments later as they approached the restaurant.

If Kassia could feel Lexie's beating heart, she would know the answer. "I–I guess so."

Kassia lifted her empty hand in a pretend toast. "Here's to a new adventure."

Lexie returned the favor as they entered. "To a new adventure."

"You girls don't have to toast now. I'll buy you a drink," a teasing voice greeted them.

"Hi, Brad," Kassia answered, giving him a big smile.

Consistent with Kassia's taste in men, Brad possessed smoldering good looks. A tan made him appear as though he spent hours in the sun, and his build indicated he might have played football in school. Lexie sent Brad a shy but pleasant smile and searched with her eyes for the man Kassia had chosen for her.

When Brad stepped aside, Lexie learned her worst fears had been confirmed. Kassia had managed to hoodwink her again.

four

Lexie caught her breath. Theo appeared even more handsome than he had the previous night.

"I see she tricked us both again," Lexie whispered to him while Brad was telling the hostess they had reservations in his name.

Theo's brow furrowed. "Tricked us?"

Seeing his apparent innocence, Lexie regretted her observation. "Isn't that just like her?" She chuckled in hopes he would know she wasn't upset. "I guess I should thank you for being such a good sport."

"Kassia didn't tell you?" He let out a breath. "I didn't want her to bring you here against your will."

Lexie cringed. She wished she hadn't made such a lame attempt at humor. Now she'd let him know she didn't want to be on this date. Even though she had no intention of finding romance at this time, if ever, Lexie knew hurting Theo's feelings wouldn't accomplish anything good. "I'm not here against my will. I agreed to the date. I even dressed up. See?" She motioned to her dress.

"I noticed." His smile confirmed the truth. Theo extracted a tissue from his pocket and wiped his nose. "Sorry."

Suddenly she remembered his allergies. In the past he would take out a tissue when he was nervous. "Poor thing. I'm sorry your allergies are acting up."

"That's okay." He shrugged then stuffed the tissue quickly in his pocket, as if to hide his embarrassment. "I can't imagine life without them anymore."

She understood what he meant. As inconvenient as they

were, his allergies somehow endeared him to her. They made him human when otherwise he seemed nearly perfect.

"You could have worse problems." Lexie smiled at him. "She told me I had a blind date, but I didn't know I'd be so lucky."

"Thanks for the thought, even though I know you don't mean it."

Lexie opened her mouth to object but was interrupted.

"Will this table be all right?" The hostess indicated the cozy booth in a corner of the restaurant. A mauve colored cloth decorated the table. Silver forks rested on matching napkins. Several glasses were set for each person, along with gold-rimmed plates. The elegant table would have been ideal—on any other night.

Lexie hesitated. Trapped or not, she realized she didn't mind being in Theo's company after all. But the thought of spending an evening with him, sitting in such an intimate, dimly lit part of the restaurant, left her with mixed emotions.

"This is perfect!" Brad and Kassia spoke in unison then broke into laughter at their mutual agreement.

Theo and Lexie rolled their eyes at each other. Their non-verbal communication sent them into chuckles as well.

Perhaps I shouldn't be so hard on Kassia. I'm being just as silly as she is.

Theo's arm bumped against Lexie's for an instant. Non-verbal communication or an accident? Either way the slight contact sent a wave of emotion through Lexie that both surprised and confused her. She immediately stepped away from him.

At the same time she realized she wanted more of his touch, however casual. She found herself imagining him taking her hand in his. How she missed being in love!

But love wasn't in the picture for her. Not now. Not yet. Even though she and Theo could build on a foundation of friendship, the memories they shared happened a long time ago. They would have to start over. Yet being with him still felt so comfortable, so right.

A male voice interrupted her musings. "You should have been at the meeting yesterday." Brad's crowing was too loud for anyone sitting at their table—or those nearby—to ignore.

"I wish I could sit in on all the big meetings," Kassia cooed. She rested her elbows on the table and propped her face in her cupped palms.

"One day you'll be in on all the action," Brad assured her.

Kassia looked at Lexie. "Brad goes to all the meetings for the bigwigs. Little ol' me just has to sit in the office by the phone all day."

"Sometimes I think I'd like to change places with you," Brad said. "You wouldn't believe the incompetent morons I have to deal with every day." He winked at Kassia. "Present company excluded, of course."

Kassia giggled.

"The Goen presentation was a mess before I showed Bob how to use the computer presentation program. He didn't even know how to put together a pie chart. Can you believe that?"

"Really? What a scream!" Kassia laughed.

"If it weren't for me," Brad said, "the whole place would shut down tomorrow."

"You're so right!" Kassia agreed.

Lexie tilted her head toward Theo and sent him an amused look. He returned the gesture.

With Kassia hanging on Brad's every word, Lexie and Theo could ignore him for the most part, particularly since his talk continued to focus on his job. Lexie was much more interested in Theo and how he'd spent the past few years— mainly making his way up his own corporate ladder. Some- how, when Theo talked shop, he wasn't boring at all. She found her attention centered on his conversation. Perhaps he was so fascinating to her because he didn't seem to boast about his accomplishments, unlike Brad. Or perhaps she and Theo had a shared history. Lexie didn't want to contemplate feelings beyond that.

As the meal progressed, Lexie not only forgot about Brad and Kassia, but she hardly noticed the food that normally she would have savored without distraction. Salmon baked in dill, lemon, and butter, accompanied by a sautéed mixture of zucchini and yellow squash, seemed to melt in her mouth. Yet Theo's company offered far more satisfaction.

Lexie knew from Kassia's glowing reports that Theo's job occupied a significant place in his life. She halfway expected him to spend most of the night talking shop while she nodded blankly or otherwise feigned both knowledge and interest. To her delight, once Theo gave her a brief rundown on his career, he didn't dwell on it. Instead he spoke about the dreams he still held—dreams she remembered he'd shared with her years ago when final exams worried them more than anything else. Despite having worked in the real world, he still possessed the charm of an idealistic student. His longings—to write a volume of poetry, to travel to exotic places, to own a vacation home—had never changed. He had lots of dreams. But none of them included what was most important to her.

She waited for him to talk about a desire to have his own family one day. After all, college was past, and Theo was now closer in age to thirty than twenty. Her waiting proved in vain. Not once did he mention marriage or the hope of one day being a father. Desperately she wanted to throw him hints. She couldn't. What would he think? Nothing would make a man run away faster than a woman who seemed marriage minded too soon. Besides, hadn't she just told herself that nothing was farther from her mind?

"Lexie," he said over his dessert, a slice of chocolate mousse cake drizzled with raspberry sauce, "I just realized

I've been a lousy dinner companion. You've let me drone on and on all night, and you haven't said a thing about yourself."

"But didn't you like having an audience?" She wrinkled her nose at him.

"Sure! Especially one as beautiful as you are." His voice caressed the words.

Where was a quick quip when she needed one? Her mouth went suddenly dry. Speaking seemed impossible. She took a drink of water.

It didn't help. Unnerved by her reaction to his compliment, Lexie set down the glass, then crushed her napkin in her fist. She became conscious of the cloth fibers and how rumpled they would become.

Not knowing what else to do, Lexie stared at her empty plate as though it were an exhibit at the Smithsonian. She felt Theo's presence draw nearer. He still wore the same citrus cologne he always did. Her memory flashed back to the one occasion they exchanged Christmas gifts, during their junior year. A phase when they were growing closer. So close she thought they might become a couple. She had bought him a bottle of aftershave. The purchase seemed extravagant at a time when her only income came from her summer job in her dad's office. But the splurge had pleased him.

Lexie inhaled softly. She had forgotten how good the fragrance smelled on him. She wanted to draw closer to him, too. She forced herself to resist.

"I know life hasn't been everything you wanted. You didn't deserve to lose your husband so young." Theo's voice conveyed genuine sympathy. He placed his hand on the table as if he would take hers.

Lexie couldn't bring herself to respond to the gesture. Instead she nodded without speaking.

Theo quickly picked up his glass and took a swallow of iced tea. "Tell me about what you've been doing lately." The intimacy had left his voice.

"Oh, there's nothing to say. Nothing nearly as exciting as the things you've been telling me." Guilt prodded Lexie. Except for the Lord, Piper occupied the center of Lexie's universe. Yet she hadn't uttered the first word about her. Usually eager to pull out Piper's photos from her wallet, Lexie kept them hidden.

Piper is part of me. Why am I so reluctant to talk about her? What is wrong with me? When she looked into Theo's eyes, she knew exactly what bothered her. *I don't care how I feel; any man who wants to get anywhere near me must know about Piper. He must accept my daughter. Even love her.*

Lexie reached into her purse. She had to find her wallet, to show Theo a picture of Piper.

At that moment Theo cleared his throat and nodded toward their companions. Lexie's eyes widened. She had noticed Brad taking Kassia's hand during the meal, but now, nestled in the corner of the booth, they had progressed to kissing and seemed no longer concerned about where they were—or who was watching.

❧

All night a vague feeling of drowsiness threatened to overcome Theo in spite of Lexie's charms, a side effect of taking two antihistamine pills a half hour before dinner. All that changed when Kassia and Brad chose to display their affection so openly.

Theo knew he shouldn't watch them and, after some minutes, finally tore his gaze away from them. He glanced sideways at Lexie. She shifted in her seat, crossing and uncrossing her legs, tugging at her dress. Seeing Lexie's beauty only reinforced in Theo's mind how much *he* wanted to kiss *her*.

Why can't I be like Kassia and Brad? What would it be like not to be saved—or at least to act that way—not to care what the Lord or anyone else thinks? What would it be like to indulge my feelings, the feelings I have for Lexie, the ones that have never died, even after all these years?

No! He wouldn't trade his relationship with Christ for all the kisses in the world. Waiting for the right woman hadn't proved easy, but Theo knew that once the Lord did lead him to his future wife she would be worth everything. Sure, Brad and Kassia were obviously enjoying themselves, but how long would their feelings last? Theo suspected they wouldn't last long at all.

Theo stole another glance at Lexie. The napkin in her lap held her attention. Why did she avoid looking at him? He sighed inwardly. Lexie showed no sign of welcoming any expression of emotion from him, a man she had been friends with for years. Otherwise she wouldn't have been so careful to avoid even the slightest touch. Although she hadn't made an issue of the fact, Theo could tell by the way she conducted herself—with the reserve of a lady—and the fact she still wore the gold cross he remembered from her student days that they agreed on spiritual matters. Life without the Lord would be nothing. Though she looked as stunning as ever, her faith made the attraction even more compelling.

❧

She waited for Theo to say or do something—anything—to keep the other couple from embarrassing them so much they could never patronize the restaurant again. Instead he watched them as though they were performing on television. She could imagine one of those parental notification boxes in the corner.

She cleared her throat. "Kassia," she managed to say, "why don't you and Brad get some fresh air?"

Theo chuckled a little too loudly at her chiding. She could tell by the strained look on his face that their friend's public display of affection with a man she barely knew made him uncomfortable as well.

For an instant a picture flashed in her mind of Theo taking her in his arms and kissing her. Lexie pursed her lips and blinked, willing the picture away.

Kassia and Brad broke their embrace. "Hey," Kassia said, "it isn't as if you two don't have lips, you know."

Lexie groaned.

"Don't worry." Brad winked at Kassia. "We can catch up later."

Kassia's giggle only served to make Lexie more anxious. Had her friend lost her mind? How could she let this strange man speak to her that way, as though she were little more than a conquest?

"I don't know," Kassia said. "Lexie is living with me for awhile. I'll have a chaperone for at least a few weeks." Kassia winked at Lexie.

Brad cast Lexie a sly look. "You say that like it's a bad thing."

Lexie crushed her napkin in her fist again.

"Apparently, Brad," Theo said, "you must not be used to hanging out with women who are ladies."

Brad raised his eyebrows. "Is that what you think?" He placed a possessive arm over Kassia's shoulders. "The women I hang out with don't need a guy to speak for them. Isn't that so, Kassia?"

"Oh, I don't know. I think Theo's being kind of cute." Kassia sent a sideways, heavy-lidded look Brad's way. "You'd defend me if I needed it, wouldn't you, Brad?"

"I'm assuming you can defend yourself. It looks to me like your mouth is working pretty well."

Lexie laughed even though Brad's humor was hardly in good taste. She was simply eager to ease the tension around the table. Kassia took the hint and joined her laughter. Theo's expression remained dark, but his jaw seemed to loosen a bit. The waiter didn't delay in presenting them with the check.

"Let me pay for my dinner," Lexie whispered to Theo.

"No way," he answered. "I invited you. Well, sort of." He grinned in the way she had seen a million times back in school. Once again, the years seemed to dissolve into oblivion.

"Are you sure?"

"Sure, I'm sure." He took out his wallet and extracted a credit card.

"Thanks." Lexie hoped her expression didn't reveal her secret relief. She needed to save every dime she could. She sent a silent prayer of thanks to the Lord that Theo still treated her like a precious jewel.

A gentleman. The word described Theo through and through. He hadn't changed a bit since college. Yet her fascination with him felt fresher than ever.

Stop it! You are not here to find a husband!

If only her feelings didn't betray her.

As did Kassia's, apparently. How could she have given everyone in the restaurant such a display, embarrassing Theo and her and surely herself by attracting the attention of nearby diners?

A few minutes later, on the drive home, Kassia broke the silence in the car. "So. How did things go with you and Theo?"

"I'm sure you wouldn't know, since you were so busy."

"Sure was." Kassia giggled. "Too bad you couldn't follow our example with Theo. He's neater than ever, isn't he?" Kassia glanced at her.

Lexie felt herself blush as she nodded.

"Admit it. You're glad I set you up with him tonight."

"Well, it wasn't the worst evening of my life," Lexie said.

Except when you made a fool of yourself.

"That's what I thought." Kassia smiled. Her display of affection with Brad had been inappropriate by almost anyone's standards. But if she felt the least bit of embarrassment, she didn't reveal it to Lexie.

Lexie sighed. Kassia had been decent—even a little on the shy side—in school. Tonight showed she must have fallen—hard and long. If Kassia jumped on every man she met, Lexie knew she should reconsider living with her. She would have to confront her friend.

She looked over at Kassia. The smile from earlier in the evening lingered on her expression. Even though her happiness resulted from a shallow type of physical love, Lexie could tell Kassia was still too enthralled to listen to reason. The confrontation would have to wait until tomorrow.

five

The next morning Lexie tried to swallow past the knot in her throat. She dreaded the idea of challenging Kassia about her behavior the previous night. How could she fall all over a man she barely knew? At least Lexie could only conclude she didn't know Brad well before last night. He worked in another department of her company, but she had admired him from afar. Kassia hadn't told Lexie how she managed to get her crush's attention—but she should have known to exercise more self-control.

She could hear the swishing of Kassia's nightshirt and padding of her bare feet on the kitchen linoleum. Thoughts of Kassia's generosity popped into her mind. She didn't expect much of Lexie—only that she share in the cooking and cleaning and contribute to the rent.

And how did Lexie plan to repay her friend? By passing judgment. By acting like a parent instead of a peer, ignoring the fact that Kassia was well past her twenty-first birthday.

Maybe I shouldn't say anything. Or maybe I should. Father in heaven, please guide me!

"Good morning!" Kassia's voice exuded cheerfulness.

The lilt could only be the result of last evening. Lexie wondered if Kassia might break into song.

"Good morning." Lexie's voice didn't match her friend's tone. "Are you always this happy in the morning?"

Okay, I know I'm grasping at straws, but—

"You know better than that!" Kassia laughed, grabbing a mug out of the cabinet and cocking her head toward the half-filled, four-cup coffeemaker. "Does that coffee have my name on it? Not that I need it today. I'm already flying."

Lexie peered into her empty cup. She had been saving the coffee for herself, but she could wait. "You're welcome to it."

"Thanks!" Kassia poured a cup of the brew. She leaned against the counter and took a generous sip. "Mmm. You've turned me on to espresso. I never thought it would be good in a regular drip coffeepot."

Lexie shrugged. "I don't know. It really doesn't taste the same."

She remembered how much she enjoyed the espresso her mom made. On special occasions, and even on some rainy Saturday afternoons, she'd brought out her collection of tiny Turkish coffee cups a friend on the mission field had given her as a Christmas gift. Lexie's favorite cup was decorated with red enamel paint that served as a background for fili-greed gold leaves. Her mom liked the white cup with a single yellow rose best.

Lexie took a sip of her beverage. "It'll have to do." She chuckled. "At least until I have several hundred dollars to blow on an espresso machine."

"An espresso machine? Have you ever seen one of those things? They're huge. I hope if you manage to save up that much money, you'll have plenty of counter space."

Lexie noted Kassia's overburdened countertops. The Euro-pean kitchen—a euphemism for "tiny" in Lexie's book—was a far cry from Mom's generous surface area that held her espresso machine with ease. "Good point."

Kassia sat down at the square pine table and reached for a box of low-fat cereal. Lexie tried not to grimace. She pre-ferred her sugary childhood favorite. She couldn't see the merit of eating cardboard flakes, no matter how few calories they contained. Besides, light flakes left her stomach growling with hunger well before lunch.

"Care for some?" Kassia teased. They had discussed cereal

choices several times. Neither one would change her mind.

"No, thanks." She tapped on the red box that remained on the table. "I'll stick with this, thank you."

"These aren't so bad once you get used to them." She lifted her spoon then brought it to her mouth as if she were trying out for a part in a commercial.

Lexie decided to ignore Kassia's jesting. "So what's on your agenda for the day?"

"Grocery shopping and errands. I'm keeping my cell phone with me all day. Brad promised to call."

"Oh. He promised, huh?"

"Yeah, I know what you're thinking," Kassia said. "You remember all about those guys who say they'll call but never do. You can spare me the lecture. I've heard it before." She wrinkled her nose. "And I've lived it a few more times than I'd like to admit."

"But you think Brad's different."

"I know he is."

Lexie was certain Kassia was deluding herself. Despite her resolve not to pass judgment, she realized she couldn't keep her feelings quiet. She braced herself for an argument. "Is he different because you work with him or because he thinks there's more where last night's actions came from. . . ?" Her voice trailed off. Lexie knew her convictions. Why did she suddenly sound so weak?

Kassia's eyes narrowed at her, and Lexie remembered why. When confronted, Kassia tended to react like a threatened viper—recoiling then striking with venom.

"What is that supposed to mean?" Kassia set her spoon down in her cereal bowl with a thump. Milk splashed on the table.

Lexie wished she hadn't started the conversation. Now that she had confronted Kassia, she couldn't back away. "I—I guess you don't realize how you and Brad looked last night. Theo and I aren't used to seeing couples kiss so openly."

There. She'd said it. Adding Theo's name made her feel more confident. Telling Kassia he shared Lexie's revulsion made her feel more justified in mentioning it.

Kassia sneered. "I should have known."

"Should have known what?"

"That if I let you stay here, you wouldn't be able to keep your opinions to yourself."

"I'm sorry."

"Sure," Kassia spat out. "Sorry I don't agree with you. I'm an adult, and I can do what I want. I did nothing wrong. You're as self-righteous as ever. I'm not Piper, and you're not my mother."

"I know—"

Kassia's eyebrows shot up. "And speaking of your daughter, what did Theo say when you told him about her?"

Lexie wished she could fall through the floor. She pressed her lips together and balled the hem of her robe in her fist.

"Well?" Kassia prodded. "Did he mind?"

"I, uh, I—I didn't tell him."

"What?" Kassia's voice rose. "What do you mean, you didn't tell him? How can you spend a whole evening with somebody and not even mention you have a daughter?"

Lexie looked down at her empty cereal bowl. "I—I just didn't."

Kassia's raised eyebrows were all the condemnation Lexie needed. Instead of retorting as Lexie expected, she ate a fresh spoonful of cereal. In her silence she expressed more graciousness than Lexie in her criticism. Lexie slumped in her chair, feeling like a hypocrite.

"Look—I know I seem like a poor excuse for a mother and a sorry example as a friend." Lexie faced Kassia's stare. "You're right. I have no business making comments on your life. But you're more than a roommate to me. You're my friend. I don't want to see some insensitive guy hurt you."

"You let me worry about insensitive guys." Kassia's icy tone demonstrated no forgiveness.

"Don't worry," Lexie said. "I'll be out of here soon. I'll be looking for my own apartment next week."

Kassia swept her hand toward the front door. "Why wait? It's Saturday. The apartment rental offices are open."

Lexie felt the sharpness of her remark. Had Kassia fallen so far that the slightest discussion about her life could dissolve their friendship?

"Brad is coming over with some DVDs tonight," Kassia added. "I doubt you'll want to be here."

Stunned, Lexie could scarcely nod. "I won't be able to rent an apartment today, I'm sure, but I'll be out of the way tonight."

Before Kassia could answer, Lexie retreated to her room. She looked around at the small room, which barely held her double bed and dresser. Hunting for an apartment when a foul mood and troubled thoughts occupied her mind would only spell trouble.

A jog. That's it. She needed a run for mental and physical therapy. She threw on a pair of black leggings, a T-shirt, and her running shoes. As she bound her hair into a ponytail, she felt better. A jog guaranteed she would forget her argument with Kassia, for a little while anyway. At least it would get her out of the apartment and away from Kassia's ill temper.

Her roommate surveyed Lexie from head to toe. "You're not apartment hunting in that getup, are you?"

"No," Lexie assured her as she headed for the door. "Maybe I'll try after my run. See you later."

"Don't take too long," Kassia said as Lexie closed the door behind her. "Some of the apartment rental offices close at noon."

"Thanks," Lexie muttered. "I'll remember that."

As soon as her feet hit the sidewalk, she reveled in her freedom. The brisk spring air felt good against her skin, and she picked up speed. She traveled swiftly through the apartment complex parking lot and headed into the adjoining neighborhoods. Though her exercise regimen kept the weight off, the sense of well-being from strenuous movement offered its own reward.

Deep in thought, Lexie jogged through one street after another. The foliage and flowers along the sidewalks varied according to whatever development, complex, or subdivision she passed through. Whether the plantings were red maples, ornamental pear trees, pines, pansies, or a combination, their expression of God's creation contrasted with the constant drone of one car after another whizzing by her. Did everyone go out on Saturdays?

Before she realized what had happened, Lexie saw that she had ventured into a different neighborhood. A stoplight forced her to jog in place as cars passed through an intersection.

"Where is this?" She looked at the street sign and realized she'd run to the entrance of Theo's development. Waiting for the light to turn, she contemplated the rooftops. Gray and black proved the most popular colors, but an occasional red roof brightened the scene. She wondered whether Theo had chosen a red roof to express his individuality, a basic black roof, or gray for the ultimate in conformity. She ventured black as a guess. The word "maverick" never described the Theo she knew.

The light turned.

"Should I or shouldn't I?" she muttered to herself as she crossed the street. "I know I shouldn't, but I'm going to. I'm going to see if Theo's home."

six

"Who can that be?" Theo wondered when he heard a knock on the door. He looked at his watch. Who would come knocking this early on a Saturday morning?

In a housing development filled with families, he guessed his caller might be a child selling cookies, magazines, or trinkets. Nothing he needed to buy. If he answered the door, he'd feel too guilty to turn down a waiflike little girl or boy in a Scout uniform. He often ended up with a box of candy or a magazine subscription he didn't need. But, if he could ignore the knocking, the young salesperson would go away.

He hoped.

Theo stared at his computer screen. He'd been at the game since he'd finished his workout earlier that morning. After putting in extra hours the previous week, he'd finally gotten caught up at work. His reward was a Saturday to himself and the rare opportunity to play his computer game. No unexpected visitor would keep him from winning.

Theo sent his character down a dark path, searching for a lost treasure. Just as the dwarf was about to enter a virtual cave sure to harbor a virtual dragon, the knocking on his real life door became urgent and punctuated by the ringing doorbell.

What could be so important? He sighed as he remembered someone even more sinister.

I hope it's not the president of the homeowners' association bugging me again.

Jack would have no qualms about using this Saturday morning to convince Theo to install a privacy fence to match his neighbors'. Something about presenting a uniform appearance.

Theo continued to resist. His reasons were hard for Jack to understand.

Each day before work Theo indulged in a cup of coffee. Often he would carry it to the deck he'd built onto the back of his house and sit in one of the green chairs he'd bought on sale at a drugstore. Watching the birds feeding and the squirrels scurrying through the yard offered him a bit of pleasure to start his day. Erecting a privacy fence would mar his view of the open space, however small. Now Jack wanted to deprive him of this pleasure. He believed uniformity would maintain property values. Theo wasn't so sure. The two of them would never agree.

How can I get out of this one?

Theo sighed as he allowed his character to be defeated by a laser blast. The punitive and powerful dwarf evaporated into a puff of white smoke. He had been so close to winning. Now Theo would be forced to start the level all over again. He paused the game.

As Theo made his way to the front door, he thought of every possible excuse not to erect a fence. Proclaiming his desire to blaze his own trail in the suburban jungle wouldn't do. He sighed. He would just have to face Jack and stand his ground.

He looked through the peephole. When he saw his visitor, he took in a breath.

Lexie!

Letting out a big sigh of relief, Theo opened the door. "What are you doing here?"

"Thanks for such a warm greeting." She smiled wryly. "I was ready to leave. I knocked and knocked before I finally found the doorbell. I wouldn't have been so persistent except I saw your car."

"I'm sorry I took so long. It's just that, well, I wasn't expecting you."

"I know." She looked away. "If this is a bad time—"

"No. It's fine." He opened the door wider. "I wasn't doing anything much."

So much for playing the cool, disinterested bachelor.

She stepped inside. "I guess I'm not following what they call 'the rules' by dropping in on you like this."

"The rules?"

"Yes. Don't you remember the book that came out with that name sometime ago? Two women wrote about the things their mothers and grandmothers told them to do and not do to get a man."

Theo made a show of rubbing his fingers against his chin in mock contemplation. "Considering I'm not trying to get a man, I guess I let that one pass me by."

She grinned. "Good point."

"Oh, so you're trying to get a man, eh?" He folded his arms and puffed out his chest.

"Don't flatter yourself," she told him. "Besides, you know me too well for any rules to work on you."

"Oh, really? Maybe you'd better tell me what they are so I can be on the lookout for some other sly female."

Lexie's eyes widened for a second before she composed herself.

Could she be just the least bit jealous? The thought was not an unhappy one.

"All right, then. I wouldn't want you to get bamboozled by a viper." She arched her eyebrow. "Let's say I just read that book and was trying to follow it. Then I'm supposed to be mysterious and unavailable most of the time."

"And you're breaking the rules how—?"

"Because here I am, dropping in the day after we had dinner out. Which I enjoyed, by the way. Oops. Just broke another rule." She chuckled. "So much for being mysterious."

"Sounds to me like those rules are worth breaking. I'd

rather you be yourself than pretend to be a mystery woman."
Theo cleared his throat. "Besides, I can't get too much of a
good thing. So what brings you here?"

"My feet. Literally." She chuckled and pointed to her running shoes. "I was out for a jog and ended up here. Somehow."

He noticed that sweat stood on her face and arms and
her T-shirt proclaimed the message "God Loves You." An
image of the two of them jogging together formed in his
mind. If only—

"That's why I don't look as nice as I'd like to," she explained.
"I guess I should have realized I'm too sweaty to visit anybody. Maybe I'll stop by another time, when I'm more
presentable." She stepped toward the door.

"No!" he nearly shouted. Then he added softly, "I mean,
you don't have to go."

"Are you sure?" She seemed relieved.

"Sure, I'm sure. Besides, I think you look just fine. Even
better than you did last night."

She gave him a quizzical look.

"I didn't mean that," he added. "I mean, you looked great
last night, too. Beautiful, in fact. Even more beautiful than
you do today." No, that didn't sound right, either. "I mean,
well—I'm not doing well with this, am I? No wonder I'm
stuck playing computer games on a Saturday morning."

She laughed. "Is that what you were doing? Playing a
game? No wonder you didn't want to answer the door. I like
computer games, too. I can start on a Tuesday night, and the
next thing I know, it's Thursday afternoon!"

"You, too? Hey, that reminds me. I'd better cut off the
game. I left it on pause." He motioned for her to follow him
into his office, which was bare except for the desk, a lamp,
some papers, and the computer.

Lexie didn't enter but hovered in the doorway. "I don't get
to play much, though."

Theo swallowed. No doubt Lexie had far too many dates to worry herself with computer games. "Well, I did work out this morning. And I plan to mow the lawn this afternoon as soon as the grass dries out. So I hope that lowers my nerd quotient." He smiled nervously.

She looked at him. "No one would call you a nerd."

He smiled at her compliment and headed for the kitchen. "In that case, may I get you a soda?"

She shook her head. "Water would be fine."

"I have some sports drinks here if you'd rather have something with a little flavor."

She didn't answer right away. "Sounds tempting, but I think I'll go with plain water. Thanks."

Theo noted she was about to follow him into the kitchen. He remembered the dishes he'd left in the sink. "Uh, why don't you make yourself comfortable in the family room? I'll be right back."

He hurried to pour her water, then entered the family room. "So, besides your feet, what brings you here?" He handed her the water and sat beside her. "To be honest, I didn't know you had my exact address. Not that I mind."

"Kassia told me. She's quite impressed with how well you've done for yourself." Lexie surveyed the room from the floor to the cathedral ceiling. "I have to say, she was right."

Theo didn't think Lexie was visiting to inspect his house and thus gauge his success. Money had never been the highest priority in her life. Otherwise, she wouldn't have married Curt after he dropped out of college his sophomore year.

"I'd show you around the house, but it's a mess." He wouldn't let anyone into the unfinished basement he used for storage. He rarely made his bed; the guest room hadn't been dusted since one of his fraternity brothers last visited; the third bedroom was piled with books. He still needed to buy a bookshelf for his collection. Why he held on to his political science and biology textbooks, he didn't know; but he couldn't bear to part with them.

And the bathrooms. Did he remember to put hand soap in the powder room? He could keep her out of the upstairs, but he couldn't deny her entrance into the hallway powder room. Uh oh.

"That's okay," she was saying. "I didn't come to see the house. I came to see you."

"Good. I hope you're not embarrassed to visit the smallest model in the development."

She glanced around the room again. "This is the smallest model? You're kidding, right? Seems pretty big to me."

"Especially for a bachelor? I bought it as more of an investment than anything else. Real estate is usually a pretty safe place to put your money."

"Nice place. Even if it is nearly empty." She laughed.

"I'm just waiting for a nice woman to come along and decorate it for me."

Theo stopped. He refused to look at Lexie. *Did I just say that?*

"Nice yard, too, I noticed."

"I hope you're not too upset that I don't live in a swinging bachelor pad."

"Why would I be upset by that?"

He shrugged. "I don't have a pool or Jacuzzi for us to lounge around in. And the neighborhood kids are always running through my yard."

"I noticed." She gulped. "You don't mind that?"

Kids. How could he answer that question without sounding like an ogre? "Funny you should say that. I thought you were a kid selling things for school or Scouts just now. That's why I didn't answer the door right away."

"You mean you can't spare a few dollars to help out the schools?" Lexie's voice was teasing.

"The first three or four aren't bad, but it seems every kid in the development stops by here. I hate to turn any of them down.

"So you're a softy after all. And a gentleman, too."

"A softy and a gentleman who could go broke buying all that stuff." He heard youthful voices shrieking in the adjacent yard. "As you can hear, they can be noisy. I'm getting used to it, but I wish they'd hold it down. You'd think they'd drive their own parents crazy after awhile."

"I like how the black roof and black shutters contrast with the white vinyl siding." She finished her water.

Huh? How did she jump from kids to siding?

"Uh, yeah," he answered. "I thought going with the basic colors was the best bet. I guess you saw some of the red roofs. I'm still not too sure about those."

Lexie chuckled. She started to set her glass on the end table, then stopped.

"Here. You can use this for a coaster." Theo handed her an old envelope. "Do you think that's what I should have gotten?"

"An envelope?" she shrugged. "Sometimes I use a CD case if I'm too lazy to get up and get a coaster. So far it be it from me to criticize."

"Oh, not the coasters. I don't have a set of those yet. They're on my 'to buy someday' list. I mean should I have gotten black shutters and white siding on the house? I couldn't have gotten a red roof and red shutters anyway." He answered his own question. "The house beside me has those, and they wouldn't allow two houses in a row to have the same color."

"Makes sense, even if it does hamper individuality. And now I also understand why they have three different shades of gray roofs here."

"It makes black seem pretty distinctive, doesn't it?" He held up his hand. "Don't answer that. I prefer to talk about last evening." His stomach tightened. This was Lexie, his friend, so why did he suddenly feel like a tongue-tied junior asking the most popular cheerleader to the prom? He swallowed and forced himself to go on. "I—I hope we can do that again soon—without Kassia and Brad."

"If we do ever go out again, it will have to be without them," Lexie said. "May I be honest with you?"

He wondered if she was about to reveal the real reason for her visit. He wished she could bring herself to say something more—romantic.

"I'm being honest with you," he managed.

"I know, but it's been awhile since we were close friends—really close friends—and I don't want to impose."

"You could never impose." He was disappointed by her aloofness. Maybe if she could get whatever it was out in the open, she'd be able to move on. "It's Kassia, isn't it?" he guessed.

She nodded. "We had an argument."

"I can imagine what happened. You said something to her about the way she acted with Brad last night, and now she's mad."

"You're right."

"Sounds like Kassia," he said. "At least she's consistent."

"Consistent?"

"Yes. I'd expect her to act that way."

"Really? I didn't know she had gone so far away from the Lord."

"Was she ever that close to Him?"

Lexie rested her chin on her hand. "I don't know. I never thought she took her commitment to Him as seriously as we did, but I also didn't think I'd see her act like that with someone she hardly knows."

As committed to Him as we were. She's talking to me as if we're on the same team. And I guess we are. Theo felt a wave of pleasure course through his veins. *Yes, we are on the same team, and she's sitting right here in my house, acknowledging that.*

"Did you?" Lexie interrupted.

"Did I what?"

"Theo? Are you listening to me at all?" Lexie asked.

"Oh. Um, yes. You were talking about Kassia."

"Yes." She dragged out the word as though she were talking to a disobedient pet. "I was saying I didn't think I'd ever see her behave as she did last night. Did you?"

"No. No, I didn't." He tried to find some way to defend Kassia. "Unless, well, she knew him better than we think."

"No. She told me she's had a crush on Brad for some time, but it's as if she's been watching him from afar, you know?"

"I know." With Lexie so close but treating him as just a friend, Theo suddenly sympathized with Kassia. "I guess they didn't do anything that goes against the world's standards."

Lexie ran her finger over the rim of her glass several times, observing the motion. "I wish I could disagree with you, but I can't. In fact, they probably showed a lot of restraint in comparison to how other couples might have acted."

"You're right. Some of the guys at my work probably would have taken her to a hotel room."

"That's what I'm afraid of. Except they won't need one," she said. "Kassia said he's coming over tonight."

"Maybe if you're a good enough chaperone, you can stop them," Theo suggested.

"I don't think so."

"I'm sorry Kassia's apparently changed since school," Theo said. "I'm not sure what happened. She's never responded well to criticism. Even constructive comments from a friend who cares about her."

"I'm not so sure she thinks I care that much. She told me to find another place to live," Lexie said.

"You're kidding!"

"No. I'm going to start looking soon."

"Too bad. I don't think she realizes what a good friend you are to her," he said. "How many of us have stayed in close contact since college? And I don't count attending the occasional homecoming."

"Not many—that's for sure," Lexie said. "It's not as if you and I even stayed in touch."

"Do you have to keep reminding me?" he asked. "But I'm hoping that can change now."

"I'm sure it will."

He smiled.

"We're in the same town."

So much for making any progress. Why is she so standoffish? Did I do something to offend her? Maybe I should ask.

Lexie was holding her cheek in her palm while she ran the finger of her other hand over the rim of her empty glass. No, this wasn't the time.

He cleared his throat. "You know, if you go back home, I'm positive Kassia will have forgotten the whole thing. She never was one to hold a grudge."

"If you were a betting man, you'd lose. I don't think she'll forgive me too soon. When I tried to talk to her about Brad, she told me to start looking for another apartment today."

"Today? That's awful!"

"I feel rotten about it. Kassia and I have been friends for a long time. I never thought a little disagreement would lead to this."

"That doesn't sound like Kassia," Theo agreed. "What will you do? Do you have any other places in mind?"

Lexie shrugged. "I don't know what to do. I have no idea what kind of place I can afford on my own."

"I thought you had a good job."

"I do. But—" She closed her mouth and shook her head. "You don't know the half of it."

Theo didn't know what to say. "Is this where I'm supposed to ask you to crash here with me?" He chuckled.

Instead of laughing, Lexie exhaled sharply. "How can you even think of that?" She rose from her seat. "I thought you were different, Theodore Evan Powers, but you're not. You're just like every other man I've ever known—except Curt."

He stood. "Now wait a minute—"

"No, you wait a minute. Here I am, trying to share a serious problem with you, trying to tell you how worried I am that this Brad guy is taking advantage of our friend, and all you can do is answer with an insult you try to pass off as a joke."

He didn't answer. Judging from her hostile reaction, he had overestimated Lexie's trust in him and the bond of their friendship.

"I'm sorry," he managed to say.

"Not sorry enough." Lexie swivelled on her heel and headed for the front door.

Theo ran behind her. "I'm not the problem here, Lexie. Your trouble is Curt's ghost. You can't expect a living, breathing man to compete with your sainted husband."

"Is that so? Well, you're wrong. Just plain wrong." Lexie turned and jogged down the porch steps.

"Wait!" Theo started out after her, but his bare feet were no match for her feet clad in running shoes. After less than a block he stopped, winded and discouraged.

What did Lexie mean? If Curt wasn't the problem, then what was?

❧

As she jogged back home, Lexie took the quickest route. For the first time in her memory the joy of running, gliding along in her shoes, sweating, the breeze offering a cooling effect, didn't melt away her problems. Rays from the sun felt hot on her hair. She became conscious of the bandage she had wrapped around her blistered middle toe. Neither the sun nor the bandage would have bothered her at any other time, but today was different. Each step brought her closer to the realization that she had argued with her only two trusted allies in her newly adopted city. How could she have made such a mistake? She could blame no one but herself for her loneliness.

Loneliness. After Curt's death, loneliness was too familiar. But was Theo right? Had she really been shutting out her chances of a new love because of his ghost?

No, no one was competing with Curt's ghost. Least of all, Theo. But how could she convince him?

You'll never convince anyone with that judgmental attitude of yours, she chastised herself.

As she often did while jogging, Lexie prayed. *Lord, is Kassia right? Am I being too judgmental? Why can't she see beyond her perceived criticism and realize I talked to her only as a friend out of love?*

She felt a sense of peace after she spoke to the Lord, but not a complete sense of well being that her prayers so often brought. This would take more time to resolve. But how much time did she have? Kassia had just told her to leave, and now she had argued with Theo.

Theo. What about him?

Time.

Time. Why was that word the only answer she got? Lexie exhaled, both from exertion and frustration.

She noticed an ice cream shop a short distance away. The pink and white sign promised a different kind of comfort. She dug into her waist pack and found her emergency five-dollar bill. Well, this constituted an emergency, didn't it? Okay, maybe just a pseudo emergency.

As she entered the ice-cream parlor, then took her place at the end of the long line, she suddenly felt guilty about indulging in such a sugary treat. She fought it. So what if it would replace every calorie she had worked so hard to burn? She would run again tomorrow. Besides, the body burns more calories after exercise, right?

Large tubs of ice cream offered an array of colors and flavors—everything from rich, dark chocolate to unreal colors of blue and pink with shapes meant to draw the attention of children. No matter how interesting or tempting new concoctions could be, Lexie never changed her mind about her favorite flavor.

An image of the United Nations delegation in New York popped into her head. If they would just sit down together and share big bowls of peanut butter brickle ice cream, perhaps they would be agreeable enough to solve the world's problems.

Lexie chuckled quietly at her silly thought.

"Lexie?"

The male voice sounded familiar, yet strange. She searched her brain to place a face with the pleasant tenor. Finally she spun around to see who had recognized her.

"Brad!"

Lexie had no desire to talk to anyone, but she couldn't dodge him now. She noticed he looked as good in shorts and a shirt with an athletic logo as he had the night before in a knit shirt and dress slacks for dinner. No one could deny Brad's handsomeness.

"So what brings you here on a Saturday morning?"

First Theo and now Brad. This question had become too popular. "Ice cream."

He looked down at her athletic shoes. "Really? I thought you came here by foot."

Lexie groaned at his corny joke, similar to the one she had used earlier with Theo.

"Makes sense, doesn't it?" His smile could have melted all the tubs behind the glass counter. "It isn't every day I run into a pretty jogger in an ice-cream store. I didn't think a woman as fit as you would eat anything but celery sticks."

"Celery sticks!" She thought about the sugarcoated cereal she had eaten that morning for breakfast. "Why do you think I have to jog?"

He laughed, somehow adding an alluring purr. Lexie could see why Kassia had been attracted to Brad so quickly. She debated whether to remind him he had promised to call Kassia but decided against it. Why encourage him?

Brad motioned to a small table that had just been vacated. "Since we're both here, why don't we eat together?"

"Makes sense, doesn't it?"

"Hey, that's my line." His eyes sparkled as he smiled. "I see you pay attention. I like that in a woman."

Could Brad make the telephone directory sound like an invitation?

They were inches from the table. In a second her chance to escape would evaporate. Yet after such an unpleasant morning Lexie wanted to linger with Brad and share conversation over ice cream. She was even willing to endure his bragging, simply to get her mind off her troubles.

Yet Brad seemed different. He had nothing to say about his work or his possessions. He didn't even complain about the exorbitant prices of skiing in Aspen or how he'd run into various celebrities on his last jaunt to the mountains. Lexie wondered if he sensed that status, possessions, and travel didn't impress her. Too committed to Piper, Lexie had no desire to claw her way to the top of a large corporation, and with her financial life in near shambles, luxury items and travel were out of the question. In the few moments they waited in line, bantering about nothing, her mood lifted. Yet she sensed an overwhelming need to flee.

"Come to think of it, I'd better be getting out of here." She made a show of consulting the wall clock. "I didn't realize it was getting so late." How convenient the truth had become!

"You plan to run and eat ice cream at the same time?"

"What better way to burn a few more calories?" she quipped. "Besides, I'll be seeing you again this evening."

"Oh?"

"When you see Kassia."

"Oh, yeah. That's right." He pointed to her playfully. "I'll be bringing over some DVDs. Tell me what you'd like to see, and I'll pick it up at the store."

Lexie could only imagine how Kassia would react if she took Brad up on his offer. "That's okay. I'm caught up on movie viewing for the time being. I'll be out anyway."

Brad's smile disappeared. "Oh. You already have plans."

This time she pointed at Brad. "And so do you."

"Just for tonight. Maybe we can get together some other time?"

Lexie waved as though she were a beauty queen riding in a parade. "See you later." She bounced out of the store, ice-cream cone in hand, and her change rattling in her waist pack.

Since she did indeed have to eat her ice cream while she walked home, Lexie didn't enjoy the indulgence as much as she would have if she hadn't run into Brad.

How could he act as though he had fallen hard for Kassia one night, then turn around and ask Lexie out the next day? She could only conclude that Brad had no intention of developing a deep relationship with Kassia.

Lexie returned to the apartment in time to see Kassia hang up the phone. She didn't dare ask Kassia to identify her caller. She hoped it wasn't Brad.

Kassia sent Lexie a half smile. "That was a long jog. Too long. Don't you know it's already past lunchtime?"

Lexie consulted the clock on top of Kassia's television set. "Oh. It sure is."

Kassia spotted the paper napkin Lexie held. "You had lunch on the go?"

"Not really. Just some ice cream."

"You must have broken even in calories then." Kassia's mouth formed a hard line. "I wish you had called. I was getting a little worried."

"Really?"

"Sure. I don't care if this is a good neighborhood. Jogging still isn't the safest activity for a woman alone, even in broad daylight."

"I know. But I'm careful." Lexie held her tongue from further comment. Kassia knew that Lexie couldn't afford a gym membership, and the complex didn't offer a workout room. What else did she expect her to do?"

Kassia folded her arms and tilted her head toward the phone. "I called Theo to see if you'd jogged by his house."

"Oh." She prayed Theo didn't reveal the details of their conversation.

"He said you stopped by for a glass of water." Kassia winked. "Sly girl."

Lexie let out a nervous chuckle. "That's all he said?"

"Sure. Is there something else I should know?" Her voice held an edge of suspicion.

"I—I did tell him I'd be leaving the apartment soon."

"Oh." Kassia looked at her feet. "I'm sorry about that. Stay as long as you want."

"You really mean that?"

"Sure. Or else I wouldn't have said so."

"Before you make any more promises, you'd better hear what happened later. I ran into Brad at the ice-cream parlor."

She gasped. "You saw Brad? Did he ask about me?"

"We mentioned you. At least I did. He wanted me to join you both tonight watching DVDs. I told him I wouldn't be here," she hastened to add.

"Sure—you can watch with us." Her flat voice held no sign she meant what she said. "It was nice of him to invite you. I'm glad he did." A weak smile lit her features. "What else did he have to say?"

Lexie didn't have the heart to tell her more. "Not much. I left as soon as I bought my ice cream. But, Kassia, if I were you, I'd proceed with caution if you decide to pursue this relationship with Brad. There's something about Brad I don't trust."

Kassia's eyes narrowed. "You're just telling me that. You wanted to accept his invitation to watch movies with us."

"No," she blurted out.

"You tell me not to trust Brad, but I think you're the one I shouldn't believe."

"Wait! I didn't mean to run into Brad. I had no idea he was at the ice-cream place. He saw me while we were standing in line."

"That I believe. But you're a smart girl, all alone in the city. You saw a chance to make a play for Brad, and you took it."

"Now look—I'll admit I enjoyed joking with Brad for a few minutes while we were waiting in line, but that was it. I promise you—I have no romantic interest in Brad whatsoever."

Kassia's lips tightened. "Then I suppose you were there talking to him about how wonderful I am, huh?"

"Forget it, Kassia. I don't need to hang out here and upset you even more. No man is worth our friendship." Lexie ventured an idea. "Look—how about if I spend the evening on my own and stay out late? Then you and Brad can enjoy your DVDs and have some peace and quiet without me here."

"That would be great, Lexie. Thanks for the offer."

seven

Lexie felt no relief as she sat in the restaurant and tried to read the book she'd brought with her, the one she'd been so eager to read. She'd hoped it would help her forget she was sitting there alone, with nothing to look forward to the rest of the evening. But she couldn't concentrate on the words in front of her. It wasn't the book; it was simply that she couldn't stop thinking about her day. It seemed as if no matter whom she had run into that day, the encounter resulted in a fight.

She'd found little reprieve in the phone call to her mother. Mom expressed her displeasure. How could Lexie have argued with a friend who had been so generous to her?

Lexie sighed. Of course she couldn't share with her the details that led to the argument. Humiliating Kassia would do no good.

A smile tickled her lips when she remembered her brief conversation with Piper. Lexie could listen to her little voice twitter about her day, how she found a cricket in the garage and wanted to adopt him, how Grammy had promised she could catch fireflies at twilight the next night, how Pops said they could go to the new kids' movie that weekend.

"I miss her so much," Lexie muttered. "I have to get my life together."

She closed her book.

I need to pray for Kassia. And, Lord, please guide me in my Scripture reading.

She picked up her Bible and turned to the seventh chapter of Matthew.

"'Why do you look at the speck of sawdust in your

brother's eye and pay no attention to the plank in your own eye? How can you say to your brother, "Let me take the speck out of your eye," when all the time there is a plank in your own eye? You hypocrite, first take the plank out of your own eye, and then you will see clearly to remove the speck from your brother's eye.'"

"Okay, Lord. You don't have to tell me twice." Lexie meditated on the words, reading them again and again. She hated to admit, even to herself, that she enjoyed how attractive Brad's attention made her feel. When she appeared in public with Piper, men looked upon her as a mother—and unavailable. Without Piper beside her, men saw her as an intriguing, complex woman. But they didn't see her in her true light; she was, in fact, her whole self when she was with Piper.

Her thoughts drifted to Curt and the times they shared as husband and wife. He valued her role as a mother but made her feel loved as a woman. Curt had never been the type of man to shower her with flowers and candy, but he'd always been there for her. She could share everything with him, from daily frustrations and victories to long held dreams of a distant future.

Lord, I miss him so much! I miss how Curt made me feel. Lord, will You send me someone who will love me as a woman?

Not an instant passed before a name flew into her mind.

Theo!

No.

Lexie felt the blood drain from her face. "But, Lord, Theo can't possibly be that man. He doesn't want children. My husband must love Piper, too."

Lexie glanced around the restaurant and noticed she was the last patron. She looked at her watch and saw how late it was. *Surely I can go home now, and I won't be disturbing them.*

She pulled into the parking lot and didn't see Brad's car. She let out a sigh of relief. *Maybe he went home early and left*

Kassia here. She tiptoed into the apartment and slipped down the hall to her room. She noticed the door to Kassia's room was closed, but it usually was when she went out or was sleeping. *I just pray she didn't do anything she'd regret later.*

The next day when Lexie woke, she momentarily forgot about the argument the previous day. Then she remembered. She had made a shambles of her life, and she could lay the blame upon no one's feet but her own. Sighing, she slipped on a summer dress, poured a cup of juice and left the apartment as quietly as she could. Maybe going to church would help clear her mind. Even if it didn't, she could depend on being uplifted spiritually.

Later, as she drove through town, she harbored no fear of running into anyone she knew during worship. The congregation met in a rented school auditorium and hoped to raise the money for a new building within five years. Lexie had not yet moved her membership from her home church, but for now, being part of the vibrant congregation filled her longing for a stable place to worship with other brothers and sisters in Christ. Originally she'd planned to attend church with Kassia but soon discovered her friend no longer went to church. The past Friday night Theo mentioned he attended a large church that televised its services. He invited her to join him there, but Lexie declined. She wasn't sure she was ready for such a large church—or to see Theo every Sunday.

Once she arrived, she settled into a padded seat in the auditorium. In no mood to talk to anyone, Lexie read a few passages from the Psalms and Proverbs while the four-piece band played contemporary Christian music. The service featured lively singing and a stirring sermon titled "Showing the Love of Jesus in the Workplace" and left her feeling encouraged and ready to face the week—at work anyway.

Being ready to face her life at home was another matter.

ра

Lexie turned the key in the lock and entered the living room of the apartment. Kassia was sitting on the couch. An open bag of potato chips lay beside her on the end table. The television blared with the voice of a woman trying to convince viewers to buy a laboratory created ruby and cubic zirconia ring. Kassia wasn't watching but instead was reading the newspaper. "Good, Kassia. You're home."

"Oh! It's you!" Kassia jumped, then waved the newspaper at Lexie. "I was wondering what happened to you."

"I went to a restaurant and had a book with me. I ended up staying really late. In fact I was the last customer to leave. And this morning I attended a service." Lexie walked toward her and picked up the remote control. "Do you mind if I turn this down a little bit?"

"Go right ahead." Kassia put the paper in her lap, then folded it in half. "I guess I should thank you for staying out late last night. Are you going out again tonight?"

"Do you want me to?" Lexie knew her voice sounded weak.

"No." Kassia paused. "I know what you're thinking. You're dying to ask so I'll just tell you. No, I didn't do anything with Brad that you wouldn't have done in my place."

After the display in the restaurant Lexie wondered. "Really?"

"Really. Not that Brad didn't try. But you're right. I made sure I didn't let myself get carried away."

"I'm glad to hear that."

"So you see, you could have stayed in, after all." Kassia averted her gaze to her feet. "I'm sorry you felt as if you needed to stay out so late last night. I shouldn't have done that to you. I let you down."

Lexie sat beside Kassia. "No, you didn't. I'm the one who should be apologizing to you. I have no business making any comments about your life. You can make your own decisions, without interference from me. And I really and truly have no interest in Brad. I don't know how many times I have to say it. Maybe I can never say it enough. I didn't mean to hurt you. It was all a misunderstanding." She ventured a smile. "I promise I won't interfere again. Girl Scout's honor." She held up three fingers as a sign of her pledge.

"Are you sure you were a Girl Scout?"

Lexie could hear the challenge in Kassia's remark but decided to overlook it. "I was a Scout for five years. Is that long enough?"

"I win then. I was in for six years." Kassia winked.

Lexie chuckled. Kassia had apparently forgiven her.

"Well, I guess I deserved your trying to tell me what to do," Kassia confessed. "I was the one who set you up on a blind date without even asking if it was okay. Payback is fair play."

"But I knew you only wanted me to be happy. You know, only true friends would care about each other so much."

"Yeah."

Lexie moved closer to Kassia, arms outstretched. Kassia leaned toward her and accepted her embrace.

"I'm here for you if you want to talk," Lexie added.

"Okay." Kassia's mouth narrowed. She studied the television. This time the woman wanted them to buy a pair of hoop earrings set with small stones of cubic zirconia.

Why won't she confide in me?

Lexie held back a sigh and excused herself. Even after she had retreated to the safety of her room, she didn't feel better.

Lexie's thoughts jumbled together as she threw some of her clothes in the hamper and folded others. *No matter what Kassia says, I can't stay here much longer. We're just too different. I have to find a new place. And soon. It's time for Piper and me to be reunited.*

Piper. The daughter she couldn't live without. But what about her growing feelings for Theo? No matter how hard she tried to deny them, she couldn't. She wished she hadn't pushed Theo away, yelling and overreacting because of a joke. She realized now that her response was nothing more than a defense mechanism, a way to keep him from getting reacquainted with her—this time as more than a friend.

I don't want to lose him.

A sense of dread filled her. What would Theo say when he met her daughter?

eight

The following Friday, Lexie sat in her cubicle at work, staring at a picture of Piper she had pinned to the gray panel facing her desk. She wished she could call her little girl, but a stack of paperwork demanded her attention.

A week had passed since her disputes with Theo and Kassia. Sharing an apartment with Kassia was only starting to feel more comfortable, although Lexie feared her relationship with her roommate would never be the same.

Theo was another matter. Why hadn't she tried to make amends with him? She knew the answer. She stared at Piper's photo, taken on her last birthday. Piper held up a blond baby doll dressed in pink. The toy, which Piper named Cinda after her favorite heroine, Cinderella, had become her constant companion.

I wonder if Piper is playing with Cinda now. I wonder if she's holding a tea party with her little pink plastic cups and saucers, pretending to serve Cinda tea and pastries.

Musky perfume wafted her way. Lexie didn't have to look to know that Jennifer, wearing her trademark scent, stood by her desk.

"Hey, what's up?" Lexie asked.

"Not much." Jennifer placed some papers on top of the pile in her *In* box. "Mr. Haynes needs these by noon on Monday."

"Noon on Monday?" Lexie sighed. "I'll do my best." She looked at her ever growing pile. "Maybe I'd better take some of this work home. It's not as if I have anything else to do."

"Sure you have other things to do," Jennifer offered. "You can go out with us girls after work, you know."

"I know. Thanks. Maybe next time."

Lexie didn't mention the real reason she avoided going out with the single women from the office. Every Monday Jennifer would share stories with Lexie about the wild times her group enjoyed as they visited local bars. She seemed to believe she and her friends were having fun, but Lexie wasn't so sure. The conflict of being in such a situation was certain to lead to arguments. After her fight with Kassia, Lexie had decided to be more careful about expressing the truths of the Bible in relation to how others chose to live. Better to be thought a snob or a loner than to be called self-righteous. When she flinched at the thought, Lexie realized how much Kassia's words still hurt.

"Are you positive? We always have a lot of fun. You're missing out," Jennifer added.

Lexie searched for a truthful excuse and found one. "Mom and Dad might call. For Piper's sake I'd hate to miss them."

Jennifer looked at Piper's photo. "I can understand that. But that's what a cell phone is for."

"I'll join the twenty-first century eventually." Lexie hoped her pleasant smile hid her real thoughts. She could just imagine her parents calling her on a cell phone, only to hear the ruckus of a bar in the background. Not to mention she couldn't swing another monthly fee on her strained budget.

Just then Jennifer's eyes widened, and she drew in her breath, leaned toward Lexie, and whispered, "Who's that?"

Lexie looked toward the entrance and saw Theo heading for her desk.

Theo!

His rapid steps mirrored the beating of her heart. "What's he doing here?"

Jennifer's eyes widened even more. "You know him?"

"Yes. He's a—a friend." Lexie's gaze flew to the picture of her daughter. She hoped Theo would notice it. That would be the perfect opening for her to tell him about Piper. On the other hand she hoped he wouldn't see it.

Coward!

Jennifer interrupted Lexie's inner monologue. "Does he have a name?"

"Huh? Oh, yes. It's Theo."

"He's just a friend? Then maybe you wouldn't mind setting us up."

"No!" Lexie said quickly. Her office mate's apparent interest sent a pang of jealousy through her. "I mean—he's an old friend from college."

"Oh. So that's how it is."

Lexie shushed Jennifer and hoped she'd take the hint to leave her desk. But she didn't budge.

"Hi, Lexie," Theo greeted her, his gaze directed only at her. "I'm glad I caught you. The receptionist told me you might still be in a meeting."

"I'm out now," Lexie said.

Wow. Any more brilliance and some honor society will be calling me to join.

"So what brings you here?"

Oh, yeah. They'll be calling any minute.

"I was wondering if you'd like to go to the Tobacco Company restaurant after work. You remember that place, don't you—the one they converted from an old tobacco warehouse?"

"Yes, I do." She hesitated. "The name used to bother me until someone explained its history." She paused again. "Do you mean after work today?"

"Yes. I mean today. Unless you have other plans."

She looked down at her simple summer dress. Yes, it would do.

"If this is a peace offering, I'm the one who should be making amends with you." Lexie heard Jennifer shift her weight from one foot to another and remembered they weren't alone. She didn't want to have this conversation in front of her coworker. Now it was too late. Jennifer was sure to ask about their argument at the first opportunity.

Theo seemed to sense Lexie's discomfort. He grinned. "I know this is short notice. I hope you don't mind."

"A lady's not supposed to accept a date for Friday that she's not invited to by Tuesday," Jennifer interrupted.

"Is that so?" Theo turned to her. "Did you read *The Rules,* too?"

"*The Rules*? What's that?" Jennifer asked.

"Never mind now. I'll explain later." Lexie sighed. "Theo Powers, meet Jennifer Figuerato."

"Hello, Theo," Jennifer said sweetly.

"Hello, Jennifer." He extended his hand. "Nice to meet you."

Jennifer shot Lexie a look. "If you don't go out to dinner with him tonight, I will."

"But I thought you said a lady shouldn't accept a date on such short notice."

"Never mind what I said." Jennifer waved her hand.

"Lucky me," Theo said. "Either way I have a date."

Lexie almost quipped that maybe Theo would be happier with the carefree, never married, childless Jennifer than he would her, a widow with a child in tow. Then she remembered the Holy Spirit's prodding and decided to accept Theo's invitation, especially after he had visited her in person to extend it. "In that case I'll take you up on your offer."

"Great!" He smiled warmly.

She looked at the clock. "I have a few more minutes here; then I'm free."

"Forget the clock," Jennifer piped up. "Go on. I'll make sure everything's set for the weekend."

"I don't know—"

"Hey," Jennifer said. "I saw you work through lunch. They owe you fifteen minutes and then some."

Lexie often worked through lunch and put in extra hours after closing time. "Oh, all right. Thanks."

"Any time."

An hour later Theo and Lexie were waiting to be seated at a table. Since Friday nights were always busy, the wait came as no surprise.

"Want to walk around a little while? Maybe some of the shops are still open," Theo suggested.

Lexie couldn't think of anything she wanted to buy, but just being with Theo, doing nothing, still sounded like fun. "Sure." Her stomach rumbled. "I'm getting hungry. I wish they took reservations so we wouldn't have to wait."

"Can't stand being with me that long, eh?" He didn't wait for Lexie to answer. "Watch the cobblestones," he warned.

"I will." Lexie glanced down at the uneven stone street and hoped she could manage in her heels. "Wonder why they never fixed this?"

"I guess whoever's in charge thinks this is part of the area's charm."

"I guess," she agreed.

Theo took her arm. "Or maybe a bunch of guys thought the rough street would be a good excuse for holding their dates closer."

Lexie giggled, partly from his observation and partly because his touch made her feel suddenly giddy.

"You know," he remarked as they passed several stores and restaurants, "I recently read a newspaper article about restaurants and their reservation policies."

"Sounds thrilling."

He chuckled. "Maybe not thrilling, but it was interesting. It said that twenty percent of the people who make reservations don't show up, even if they call to confirm a few minutes ahead."

"Wow! That's hard to believe."

"The restaurants run on such a slim profit margin that some of them don't like to take reservations. The lines and the wait just add to their cachet," Theo explained.

Lexie thought for a moment. "I can see that. If people think everyone wants to get in, the place seems more desirable."

"Right. Plus they can fill tables as soon as they are vacant, instead of having to wait for the reservations to show up."

"I hadn't thought of it that way." Lexie glanced up and down the street. "Looks as if they have plenty of turnover at the restaurants on this street."

"And we were willing to wait."

Lexie didn't want to admit how little she minded, as long as she could enjoy Theo's company. She peered into the window of an antique shop. "Look at that pin cushion."

"Interesting." He nodded. "Too bad they're already closed. I might have picked up a trinket for Mom."

"She likes antiques?"

"Yes, but she has her limits. Anything she has to dust has to be pretty special."

"I'm sure anything you pick out is special to her."

"I try." He grinned. "Her birthday is next month. Maybe we can come back sometime, and you can help me pick out something."

The idea that Theo thought of them together in the future gave her a pleasant feeling. "Are you sure you want me to? I mean, after last Saturday. I'm sorry I flew off the handle."

"I know. You've been under a lot of pressure, starting a new life. I'm just glad you agreed to come out with me tonight. Especially on such short notice."

Lexie didn't want to answer with more than a smile. With Theo's arm around her, she knew she didn't care when or where they were or how long in advance he asked. As long as they could be together. She didn't want the moment to end. All she wanted to do was think about the present.

The future, and its complications, could wait.

Later Lexie looked around the busy restaurant. White linen tablecloths and napkins and elegant place settings awaited customers who looked forward to fine food. A large group of people who seemed to be members of a wedding party occupied several long tables in a more secluded section of the restaurant. Their presence added a festive air. The atmosphere was just what she needed.

After they prayed over their meal, Lexie kept looking for a chance to talk about Piper. She knew she had to tell Theo about her daughter. Why was she so fearful? Theo may have thought he didn't want children at one time, but surely he would change his mind once he met Piper. Surely he could find love in his heart for her little girl. She just knew it.

Yet, as dinner progressed, Lexie realized why she'd felt so much fear.

"Of course I don't want to take off much time from work now, not with the new house and everything," Theo said as he cut into his steak. "But I'm working on building up enough leave so I can take a sabbatical one day."

"A sabbatical? Do they let you do that?"

"I don't know if they call it that. Maybe a leave of absence." Theo shrugged. "But they let you accumulate some time off to use as you like."

"That sounds good. I guess you'd use the time to travel and write poetry?"

"Sure would." He smiled.

Lexie thought about what she would do with a sabbatical. Spending unlimited time with her daughter at home sounded wonderful to her. "Or maybe you could write a travel book." She took a sip of coffee.

"A travel book." Theo laughed. "Makes sense."

Lexie smiled. Theo always laughed at her lame humor, something she cherished.

He reached over and took her hand in his. The warmth of his hand connecting with hers made Lexie tingle. She wondered if perhaps Theo could occupy a special place in her life.

He looked at her. "How would you like to be my secretary?"

She let out a nervous chuckle. "Oh, I don't know."

"You'd be a good one. Didn't you tell me you type eighty-five words a minute?"

"Just you, me, and the laptop computer, all alone in the wilderness?"

"Sounds good."

"Can we bring anyone else along?"

He seemed surprised. "Why would we want to?"

Lexie looked down at her empty plate and withdrew her hand. No way would Piper or any other child ever fit into Theo's dreams.

"What's wrong, Lexie?" Theo asked.

She shook her head. Why did Theo always sense her changing moods? Every time they talked, she felt as though they had picked up where they'd left off the previous time.

"What's the matter? Are you homesick?"

Lexie nodded. "You could say that."

"You'll feel great after dessert. A good dose of chocolate cures everything. Even homesickness."

His comment enabled her to skirt the issue. She did miss her home, but she missed Piper more. "How do you know about being homesick?" she asked. "Your family lives less than a hundred miles from you. You can see them any time you want."

"Yeah, we're still pretty close. But I'll take plenty of chocolate with us on our trip anyway." He grinned. "In the meantime I wonder what the waiter will tell us they have for dessert tonight."

"I don't care for dessert. May we just go home?" She knew politeness dictated she offer to wait for him to eat dessert if he wished, but she had passed the point of caring about etiquette.

Why am I such a coward? I should have said something about Piper in the first few minutes I saw Theo again. Now it's too late. He won't understand why I haven't mentioned her. He'll think I'm a horrible mother. Maybe I should just forget this whole thing. Theo would be better off without me. Then he can live out his dream, unencumbered. Let some other lucky woman share his life.

"Lexie? Are you okay?" Theo asked.

"I'm all right. Let's go home."

Heavy silence filled the car on the way home. Lexie knew Theo thought the food hadn't agreed with her and that illness kept her from speaking. She decided to take advantage of his inaccurate conclusion. She didn't feel like talking.

Once home, Lexie was turning her key in the lock when suddenly Kassia opened the door. Horror mixed with relief covered her features.

"Lexie! I'm so glad you finally got here!" A look of fear crossed Kassia's face.

Lexie's words tumbled out. "What is it, Kassia?"

"Your parents called. They just took Piper to the hospital."

nine

Theo didn't say a word. He could only stand there and wonder what had transpired.

Piper? Who was Piper? Whoever she was, her significance in Lexie's life was obvious by the way Lexie ran to the phone in the kitchen.

With both women in a frantic state, Theo could see no point in waiting to be invited in. He stepped inside the door and shut it behind him.

Kassia was looking toward the kitchen, even though neither of them could hear Lexie's conversation from where they stood. "I hope Piper's okay." She seemed to be talking to the air rather than to Theo. "I don't know what would happen to Lexie if she got seriously hurt." She paced back and forth.

He drew in a breath. "Uh, this might sound strange, but who is Piper? And why is she in the emergency room?"

Kassia turned toward him. Her mouth dropped open. "You mean she didn't tell you tonight, either? She hasn't said anything after all this time?"

Kassia's remarks made Theo even more uneasy. Why would Lexie feel the need to hide someone from him? "Uh, no."

"Sorry. I just thought Lexie would have told you at dinner tonight." Kassia pointed to the couch. "You'd better sit down."

Theo felt a knot form in his throat. At the moment his feet didn't feel like moving. "I'll stand—thanks."

"I'll be glad to sit." Kassia dropped onto the couch, then looked up at Theo. "I can't believe she didn't say anything. Maybe I shouldn't, either." Kassia stared at her feet.

"You might as well tell me. I'm going to find out sooner or

later." He glanced toward the kitchen. "From the looks of things Lexie is in no condition to tell me herself."

Kassia nodded. "All right then. I'll tell you." She took in a deep breath but kept her gaze on her feet. "Piper is Lexie's little girl."

Theo didn't speak for a moment. He wished he'd taken Kassia's advice. He looked about for a seat, then sat on the chair beside the couch. He stayed at the edge of the chair and leaned toward Kassia. "Little girl? Lexie has a little girl?" His voice was strained.

"Yes."

Theo performed a few mental calculations and decided Lexie's daughter couldn't be more than six years old. How could he ever cope with a young child?

He gulped. "How old is she?"

"She's four."

Four. Was that better or worse? He didn't know. Theo was the youngest in his family and the only boy at that. He didn't know enough about children to have any idea other than Piper was somewhere between diapers and talking back to her elders.

A child? He hadn't counted on Lexie's bringing a child into the picture. And a girl at that. Theo could imagine connecting on an emotional level with a boy, but a little girl? His sisters had been older by the time Theo was aware of their existence. Now that two of them were married and had presented their parents with three grandsons so far, Theo's role as a fun-loving uncle consisted of giving his young nephews the latest expensive toys at Christmas and mailing a U.S. savings bond to mark the passing of each birthday. He felt ill equipped to deal with a little girl.

Embarrassment and anger soon replaced his fear. How could Lexie have let him talk on and on about the adventurous life he wanted and not say the first word to him about someone so important to her? He knew Lexie's days as a carefree coed had passed when she moved back to town. He was well aware that losing her husband at such a young age would change her forever. He had already thought about how Lexie's recent past would affect their renewed relationship, and he had come to terms with the fact that he could—and would need to—take Lexie as she now was if he wanted to be in her life.

But a little girl! He had no idea Lexie brought with her a child who would need years of intense parenting. Theo tried to imagine himself as a father. He hadn't given much thought to having children. How could he, with no romantic prospects on the horizon? Ever since he lost Lexie to Curt all those years ago, Theo had neglected his romantic life, throwing himself into his job. The monotony was relieved only by his dreams. Dreams of exotic travel and adventure. He would fictionalize his travels in a great novel that would sell millions of copies. Then he would be rich and live out his well-earned freedom.

With Lexie back in his life, old feelings had resurfaced. He realized what an emptiness he felt after losing her. An emptiness he wanted to fill. But to overflowing with a child, too? His plans for travel and adventure didn't include kids—certainly not now, perhaps never. And being a dad to someone else's child? Especially Curt's child—his nemesis from college—the man who stole Lexie from him in the first place. The thought had never occurred to him. At this point the idea seemed inconceivable.

How could I possibly manage such a thing? Reuniting with Lexie and now having to get acquainted with a child. It's too much. Piper's situation isn't ideal, since she's lost her father. What if Lexie, in misguided compassion, overcompensated and spoiled her rotten?

Theo, as insecure as he felt, couldn't stop thinking about the negative side.

What if Piper doesn't like me? What if I don't like her? Aren't relationships hard enough with just two adults? But a child, and a girl at that. . .

Camping trips, being a Scoutmaster, playing catch, teaching his son how to fish—the images that passed through Theo's mind didn't include activities a girl would likely enjoy. He pictured himself failing in trying to raise a girl. The word "failure" was not a welcome addition to Theo's vocabulary.

Not to mention Lexie's own failure to tell him the truth. How could she let him go all this time without the first peep that she had a child? How could he ever trust her again? And if he could not, how could they hope to build a lasting relationship?

The urge to walk out of the door at that moment and leave Lexie overcame him.

"Theo!" Kassia snapped her fingers in front of his face. "Yoo-hoo! Are you still in there?" Her cockeyed look told him she was only half joking.

He nodded as he awoke to the present.

"I know this is a shock."

"That's an understatement."

Kassia settled back onto the couch. "Try to look at this from Lexie's viewpoint. She didn't want to scare you off. I'm sure that's why she didn't say anything."

"Then when did she plan to say something? On our wedding day? Or on the honeymoon?"

"Huh?" Kassia's eyes widened. "Are you saying you're thinking about marriage?"

"I don't know. Did I say that?" He couldn't believe he'd uttered such words out loud. Had he indeed been thinking of Lexie in such permanent terms? His rapidly beating heart told him he had, whether or not he admitted it to himself.

"It sure sounded like it."

"Don't hold me to anything I might say tonight. I'm

too upset to think straight. Maybe I should just leave." He searched his pocket for his car keys.

"No, don't do that. That's the last thing Lexie needs right now. She's upset enough as it is."

At that moment Lexie entered the room. "If you're talking about me, you're right." Theo turned to Lexie and saw that her face held no color. Fear filled her eyes. Even though he was still angry, Theo had to resist the impulse to cross the room and take her in his arms and tell her everything would be all right.

"What happened?" Kassia asked.

"Well, you know how curious Piper is." Lexie stopped herself. "Theo. You don't know who Piper is, do you?"

"I do now," he said evenly. "Kassia just told me."

"I'm so sorry. I should have told you. I wanted to. It's just that the time never seemed right."

A number of retorts flickered through his mind, but Theo knew he would regret voicing any of them.

"I'm sorry, Theo. I shouldn't have been such a coward. I—I just didn't want to spoil—" She shook her head. "Never mind."

Spoil the moment? Is that what she was thinking?

Theo remembered how he had talked nonstop on every occasion they had been together. Even though Lexie's failure to tell him about her daughter still left him disturbed, his own emotions could be dealt with at another time. Now they needed to focus on Piper and her safety.

"You two can work out whatever is going on between you later," Kassia interrupted, expressing Theo's thoughts. "I want to know what happened to Piper."

"She got into Mom's purse and swallowed some of her headache pills. As soon as they found out, they called poison control, then took her to the emergency room."

"Did she lose consciousness?" Theo asked.

"No, praise the Lord," Lexie said.

"Is she going to be all right?" Kassia and Theo asked in unison.

"I think so. They induced vomiting, and now she's in the hospital. They're keeping her overnight for observation."

"I'm sure your parents will call as soon as they know something more," Kassia said.

"No. I don't want to wait. I want to go home." Lexie reached for her purse, which she had dropped on the floor beside the couch in her haste to call. "In fact I'm leaving right now."

"You're in no condition to make such a big trip alone," Theo said, watching her. "What is it, three hours from here?"

"Yes, that's about right."

Compassion filled Theo. Clearly Lexie shouldn't make such an anxiety ridden journey without someone by her side. "No way am I going to let you drive such a long way alone. I'll take you home myself."

She looked at him and straightened her shoulders. "No. Thank you, Theo, but Piper is my problem, not yours."

"She's not a problem." Theo's words defied his most recent thoughts, but he had to help Lexie, whether she wanted him to or not. "I insist."

"He's right," Kassia urged. "You should let Theo drive you. I'd offer, but I promised to go in to the office tomorrow to help Mandie prepare for her big meeting on Monday. She'll kill me if I renege on her."

"That's okay, Kassia," Lexie said.

"Then there's no reason why I shouldn't go," Theo said.

Lexie's lips were trembling and her eyes moist as she looked back at him. "You don't have plans, Theo?"

"I didn't promise my boss I'd be at work tomorrow. And I don't have much of a life outside work." He smiled at her. "Sure, I'd be glad to take you home."

"Well, all right." Her voice was soft. "My nerves are shot. And I sure would like the company."

❧

Theo exited onto Interstate 85 at Petersburg, grateful that light traffic enabled him to travel at a reasonable clip. The tires made hypnotic bumping sounds as the car hit pavement gaps. The trip offered little in the way of scenery except for an unbroken highway and dark stands of trees that were scarcely visible at night. Green and white signs promised a town at the next exit, and more signs announced the inevitable fast food restaurants at each stop. He wished he could have a conversation with Lexie, but she barely said a word.

He thought about confronting her, but he knew questioning her now would be a mistake. Initial feelings of anger and betrayal had dissolved to the lesser emotion of hurt, but he still couldn't rely on himself not to say something he might regret. A question nagged at him. Why hadn't Lexie trusted him enough to tell him about Piper?

Maybe the problem isn't her, but you.

The thought didn't make Theo feel any better. But what if he was the problem? Did Lexie see him as selfish, in both his dreams and the way he dominated their time together?

Whenever he faced fear and doubt, Theo knew he needed to pray. He decided to invite Lexie to join him. "Lexie?"

"I don't need to stop, thanks." She didn't turn her gaze from the passing trees.

Theo remembered they'd just passed a sign for a rest area. "That's not what I was asking. I thought you might like to pray."

"Oh." She nodded. "Okay."

Together they sent up their petitions to the Lord, for a safe trip to and from North Carolina, for Piper's recovery, for Lexie's parents, and for Lexie. As they prayed, Lexie placed her hand on his right shoulder. He felt strength in her light touch. Her faith had deepened since they had been school friends. The college coed had apparently matured into a woman. A woman of God.

Theo hoped the prayer would lead to a discussion, but he was disappointed. Instead Lexie leaned back away from him and continued to stare out the window.

He concentrated on the road for another hour until she finally spoke.

"Theo, I don't deserve you. I'm the worst mother in the world and a poor excuse for a friend. I should have told you about Piper right away."

"I've been thinking, Lexie. I admit I was hurt that you didn't trust me enough to tell me about her from the start." Theo glanced her way and noticed she opened her mouth to speak. He rushed on. "But there probably never was a good time, or at least not an ideal time. I know I've talked a lot since we've been seeing each other again."

"I wouldn't say that." Her voice seemed weak.

"Thanks for the thought, but we both know it's true. I've been talking a lot about my future plans, and you probably thought they couldn't include a little girl."

"It wouldn't be easy to traipse around the world to all sorts of exotic places with a preschooler."

"Wow! I guess I did sound self-centered."

"Why shouldn't you be?"

Lexie's answer surprised him. "What do you mean?"

"You're a single man with no ties. You have a right to enjoy your freedom now, before you take on a wife and family."

She spoke softly, as if to console and forgive, but her words only made him feel guilty. Yet her gentle ways were part of why he had been so eager to see her again when she returned to Richmond. And she had just made him realize he didn't want to think of himself, and only himself, forever.

He decided to talk about something else.

"I have something to ask, if you don't mind," Theo said gently.

"As if I have a choice," Lexie said and glanced at him, a slight smile on her lips. "I don't think I have the energy to jump out of the car."

Theo laughed. "I was wondering why you didn't bring Piper with you to Richmond. Don't you miss her?"

"You have no idea how much I miss her!" Lexie sighed and fell silent for a time.

After some moments Theo looked over at her. A tear fell down her cheek. "I'm sorry. I didn't mean to upset you."

"No, you didn't. It's been an upsetting day for all of us."

"You don't have to answer me now."

"No. I want to." Her voice strengthened with determination. "You need to know if you're going to be with me and my family." She paused. "Mom and Dad agreed to take Piper for a couple of months while I established myself in Richmond. We all thought it was a good idea, especially since I'm sharing an apartment with Kassia. She's not used to kids."

Theo snorted. "I know. If Piper was around, Kassia couldn't have any more dates with Brad—that's for sure."

"Don't even mention his name."

Her voice held an edge that piqued his curiosity, but he decided not to press for more information. "Okay. I won't."

"Tonight made me realize something. I'm more than ready for Piper to come and live with me," she said. "Even if it means losing you."

ten

Lexie sank deeper into the bucket seat of Theo's sports car. She glanced sideways at him. His eyes were wide and his body tense. Her admission had made an impact. She groaned inwardly and fixed her gaze on the trees alongside the road as if they were the most fascinating she had ever seen.

What's the matter with me? How could I have been so careless?

She had all but admitted to Theo that she loved him! With the commotion of leaving Piper, moving to a new location, living with Kassia, and renewing her friendship with Theo, Lexie hadn't thought through the repercussions of a new romantic relationship. Yet no matter how hard she tried to resist, she seemed to be chasing Theo full throttle.

Her thoughts turned to Piper. What kind of mother would she be if she weren't fully committed to her daughter, especially since she had been responsible for her father's death? No way would she commit to any man who didn't love Piper.

But you haven't given Theo a chance to love her, have you?

Lexie swallowed. She couldn't tell how Theo was handling the news. Always the gentleman, he would naturally offer to drive her to the hospital. She couldn't read through his tight expression as he concentrated on the road or figure out what his feelings were—toward her or the idea of Piper.

The knot grew in her throat. But what was she afraid of? Maybe she wasn't fearful for herself, but for Curt and his memory?

Will Theo try to take Curt's place in Piper's life? Or am I jealous of anyone who might take part of Piper away from me?

Now you're being as self-centered as Theo!

She let out a groan.

"Is my driving that bad?" Theo asked.

She felt embarrassed he had heard her. "Not so far."

"So far so good then." Theo pointed to the exit sign for Route 1 to Raleigh. "Is this it?"

"Yes. This is the one."

Lexie thanked the Lord silently for Theo's graciousness—and for their imminent arrival at the hospital.

Only forty miles now.

The hospital. She knew her job offered some type of health insurance, but Lexie hadn't studied the policy enough to know the details. Besides, had she been working there long enough for her benefits to start?

A picture of the pile of bills on her desk passed, unwanted, through her mind. She shook her head to dismiss the image as she shut the car door behind her and walked toward the hospital's pediatric unit.

Lexie swallowed hard to fight the dryness in her throat. She wished she had the courage to take Theo's hand. She longed for his supportive touch, but reaching out for his comfort seemed too much to ask at the moment.

Lord in heaven, please let Piper be okay.

She stepped quietly into the room. Her mother was reading the newspaper in the only chair. Even though the hour was late, Piper sat up in bed, watching television. She held a stuffed bear Lexie didn't recognize. She guessed the toy was a gift from her parents. To Lexie's relief, Piper looked like the happy little girl she was, full of energy. Only the beeping monitor beside her bed indicated anything was amiss.

"Piper!" Lexie hurried across the room.

"Mommy!" Piper exclaimed, reaching out for her mother.

Lexie swept her daughter into her arms. How she had missed Piper! Tears flowed down her cheeks, but she did not care.

Finally she released Piper and looked into her face. "How are you feeling, Sweetie?"

The little girl nodded. "Okay now. They made me drink some yucky stuff, and I threw up." Piper scrunched up her nose and rubbed her tummy.

"A charcoal shake." Mom folded the paper, set it on the table beside Piper's bed, and stood. "I'm so sorry this happened, Lexie." She crossed the room and hugged her daughter. "I feel it's all my fault. I shouldn't have left my headache medicine out where Piper could get to it."

"Never mind that, Mom. I'm just glad Piper seems to be okay?" She ended with a question in hopes her mom would reassure her.

"She's going to be fine, I'm sure. As I told you earlier, they're just keeping her overnight for observation." Mom stroked Piper's head. "Isn't that right, Sweetie?"

"Right, Grammy. When can I get up?"

"Not yet." Mom chuckled and looked at Lexie. "That's a good sign."

"It sure is," Lexie agreed.

Her mother took her aside, although they didn't leave the room. She lowered her voice. "The medicine she took affects the heart, and they want to be sure Piper's is okay before they release her."

"Her heart?" Lexie's own heart started pounding.

"I really don't think the doctor's worried about it. Nothing dramatic has happened since you called. I'm sure she'll be fine. It's just a precaution." Mom put her hand on Lexie's shoulder. "I'm worried about you now, Lexie. You look so tired. How are you doing, Honey?"

"Better—now that I'm finally here." The two women embraced again. "Where's Dad?"

"He's gone to the vending machines for a soda. He'll be back soon. How was the trip?"

The trip! Lexie had forgotten about poor Theo. Unwilling to overwhelm Piper, he had volunteered to stand in the hallway until they exchanged their greetings.

"I was so worried about you," Mom continued, "driving all that distance by yourself and in a car that's not so reliable. I prayed for you the whole time."

"Thanks, Mom. But I wasn't by myself."

Her mother's features softened. "Good. Kassia came with you. Where is she?"

"Not Kassia, Mom. Theo."

Her eyebrows raised. "Theo?"

"Theo Powers. You remember him. He was one of my friends from college."

She was quiet for a moment. "Yes, I think I do remember. You know, I think he liked you, but Curt stole your heart."

Lexie felt heat rise to her cheeks. "Mom!"

"Well, it's the truth, isn't it?"

Sure, Theo had always been there for her in college, but she hadn't thought of him romantically. When she met Curt in an informal study group, though, his boyish ways and handsome face captivated her. Soon they were a couple. In her self-absorption she hadn't taken Theo's feelings into consideration. Could Theo still harbor disappointment after all these years?

"What?" Piper interrupted. "Did Daddy steal something?"

Lexie's mother laughed. "No, Sweetie. It's just us grown-ups talking. Don't pay any attention to Grammy."

Piper folded her little arms across her chest. "I never get to know about any of the good stuff."

Lexie and her mother laughed, but Lexie's thoughts soon turned serious. The little girl said she didn't remember her father, but through family conversations, photographs, and videotape, he remained in memory. Though the Lord chose to take Curt home early, Lexie made sure Piper knew that both of her fathers—earthly and heavenly—loved her very much.

She choked back a lump in her throat. "Speaking of paying attention, I'd better let Theo know he can come in now."

"Yes," Mom agreed. "Let's not leave the poor boy standing out there all night."

"Is Theo the friend you and Grammy were talking about?" Piper asked.

Lexie nodded. Sometimes she wished her daughter didn't have a talent for hearing every word not meant for her ears. "Do you mind if I bring him in to see you? He drove Mommy all the way here from Virginia."

"Did he bring me a toy?"

"Piper!" Lexie and her mother admonished in unison.

"You can't expect people to bring you gifts all the time. Your mommy should be gift enough for you," Mom added.

Piper looked down. "I'm sorry."

Lexie patted Piper's hand. A small twinge of guilt pricked her. "I wish I could have brought you a gift myself, Honey; but it's late, and we didn't want to take the time to stop. We wanted to be here with you."

"That's okay."

Children. How easily they forgive.

Lexie smiled uncomfortably. This meeting wasn't happening the way she had hoped, but hiding Theo and Piper from each other any longer didn't feel right.

Lord, I know this is selfish, but I pray it's Your will for them to like each other.

Lexie crossed to the door, stuck her head outside, and looked down the corridor for Theo. She recognized him by the reddish-orange hue of the camp shirt he had changed into before the drive. The color contrasted with the blue wall he leaned against as he absently watched nurses coming and going about their business.

"Theo," she said in a stage whisper, motioning for him to come closer.

His face lit up on seeing her. She smiled in return. As she watched him approach, she couldn't help but reflect on how he always conducted himself as a gentleman. He easily could have listened in on the conversation she had just shared with her mother. Remembering what Mom had said about him, Lexie felt grateful he didn't overhear.

"How is she?" he whispered as soon as he came within earshot.

"She seems pretty happy. Are you ready to meet her?"

"Sure, I guess." He swallowed.

Lexie took his hand and gave it a squeeze. "She'll like you. I just know it." She didn't want to let go of his clasp but decided that entering while holding hands with a strange man might be too much for Piper. She kept a smile on her face as she walked into the room with Theo.

Piper looked up at Theo when he came in but had no particular expression on her face. Lexie thought she would re-introduce him to her mother first so Piper wouldn't look upon him as an intruder. "Mom, you remember Theo Powers."

A warm smile lit her face. "Yes, I do. How are you, Theo?"

"Mrs. Downey." He gave her a polite nod and a shy smile.

Ignoring the butterflies in her stomach, Lexie motioned toward her daughter. "Piper, I have someone I'd like for you to meet. This is Mr. Powers. He drove me here tonight."

"You mean Theo?"

Lexie felt her face flush, but Theo chuckled. "So they've been talking about me, eh? Did they say all good things?"

Piper thought for an instant, then shrugged. "I dunno."

The adults laughed. Lexie noticed Theo was smiling warmly while he watched Piper. She felt a sense of relief.

Piper held up the brown teddy bear Lexie had seen earlier. "How do you like my new bear?"

"He's cute. Did they give him to you here at the hospital?" Theo asked.

"It's not a him. She's a her," Piper corrected him.

"Oh. I'm sorry. Did they give her to you here at the hospital?" Piper nodded. "I named her Peanut Butter."

"How about that? She *is* the color of peanut butter," Lexie noted.

"Peanut butter is one of her favorites," Mom explained to Theo. "I think she'd eat it every meal if we'd let her."

"Yeah!" Piper agreed. "They gave me a really bad drink. It was dark and yucky. They said I had to drink it. Then I threw up." She gave her mother a pleading look. "You won't let them make me drink that anymore, will you, Mommy?"

"I don't think you'll be needing it anymore."

"Good. It was awful." She grimaced. "But I feel better now," she told Theo.

"Good," he said.

Piper turned to Lexie. "I'm sorry, Mommy."

"Sorry? Sorry for what?"

"For makin' Grammy have to take me to the hospital. And for makin' you come back."

Lexie hugged her daughter. "I'm sorry you feel bad, but I'm not sorry I came back. I missed you."

"Every minute?"

"Every minute." Lexie hugged Piper again. "You know, I was so busy making sure you're doing okay that I never asked—why did you swallow Grammy's pills, Honey? I thought I had taught you better than to go in her things and eat something without permission."

"I know." Piper looked down at the blanket covering her. "But they were pink, and I thought they'd taste like strawberries. Or maybe watermelon." She glanced up and wrinkled her nose. "I sure wish they had. They were awful! How can you eat those, Grammy?"

"When you're in pain, you'd be surprised what you might be willing to swallow. But I only take one at a time, and I don't chew them," Mom answered.

"I know you upset Grammy very much," Lexie told Piper.

"I already told her I didn't mean to upset her," Piper said.

"She did," Mom agreed. "I know you didn't, Honey. The main thing is, I hope you learned your lesson."

"I did. When can I go home?"

Lexie sat on the bed beside Piper and took her hands in her own. How small they felt! The difference in Piper's hands and her own emphasized how much Piper depended on her. She made a silent promise never to leave her little girl again.

"You can't go home tonight."

"I can't? Why not?"

"The doctors and nurses want to make sure you're okay now."

"But I feel fine!" Piper protested.

"And I'm so glad you do. But they just have to make sure. That's their job. I know you don't understand all about it now, but you will someday." She squeezed Piper's hand. "I'm sure you'll be going home first thing tomorrow morning."

"Are you gonna stay with me?"

"Of course I am. I wouldn't think of leaving."

"Yay!" Piper wiggled up and down, causing the EKG cables to pull against the heart monitor. "Can we stay up late and watch television?"

"You're already up way later than you should be." She stroked her daughter's forehead.

"I let her stay up since I knew you were coming," Mom explained.

"Can I still stay up?" Piper asked.

"We'll see."

Piper pouted. "That means no."

"No, it means I'll have to think about it."

"That still means no." Piper folded her arms. "Is that my punishment for takin' Grammy's pills?"

Lexie thought for a moment. "No, I'm not going to punish you. I think you've learned your lesson. All of us have been through enough."

"Yay!" Piper leaned over and hugged her tightly.

Lexie stroked her hair. Touching her soft curls made her realize how much she missed being home.

A familiar male voice interrupted. "Here's my little girl!"

Lexie turned to face her father. "Dad!" She rose from the bed and gave him a hug.

"How's my big girl by now?" he asked Piper.

"Fine!" She beamed.

"Good." He tilted his head toward Lexie, then toward the door.

"We'll be right back," Lexie assured Piper as she followed her father.

Mom waited for them both in the hall. "Are you all right?"

"Fine, now that I've seen Piper."

Mom placed a hand on her shoulder. "I'm so sorry about what happened. I couldn't believe it. I was in such a panic."

"Piper told us her stomach hurt," Dad said. "It took us awhile to get her to admit she'd taken some of your mother's pills."

"I feel so guilty. I had no idea Piper would be interested in my pills. I know now I should have kept them better secured." Tears moistened Mom's eyes. "The bottle had a childproof cap. I just don't understand it."

"I know, Mom. She's a curious little bird. If anyone is to blame, it's me. I should have remembered to tell you she learned how to open the caps early. Don't ask me how. I've always known to keep all medicines out of her sight." Lexie shook her head. "Apparently when she saw the color of the pills, the temptation was too great."

"She's a smart girl, that one is." Her dad puffed out his chest. "Takes after her old grandpa."

"Maybe so." Lexie giggled. She jumped slightly when she sensed someone's arm slip around her shoulder. She turned and saw it was Theo's. How wonderful it made her feel, so secure and protected. She had forgotten how such a touch felt. Lexie reached for his hand, touching his strong fingers, and smiled at him. The tiredness in his eyes disappeared, and he grinned in return.

She peeked at her mother. Her arched eyebrow indicated the gesture hadn't gone unnoticed.

After a few moments of easy conversation during which Theo became reacquainted with them, Mom pulled Lexie aside.

"Do you need any help getting your things to the room?"

"No, thanks. Theo brought my overnight bag in for me. The rest is in the car."

"Speaking of Theo, I couldn't help but notice the two of you seem to be more than friends."

Lexie felt her cheeks grow warm. "I wouldn't say that."

"Are you sure? What are your feelings for him?"

"At this point I'm not sure I can talk about my feelings about anything. So much has happened." Lexie realized she meant not only the evening's events with Piper, but also how fast events had occurred since her move. "Try not to worry about me. I want to be a blessing to you, not a burden."

"You never have to worry about that. I think of you and Piper every time I read Proverbs. 'Children's children are a crown to the aged, and parents are the pride of their children'." She looked into Lexie's eyes. "But that doesn't mean I don't worry." Her gaze rested on Theo. Still engrossed in conversation with Dad, he didn't look her way. "Curt was so good to you. He worked so hard to give you and Piper everything he could, and then there was the accident. . . ."

Her voice trailed off, leaving any other thoughts unspoken.

"I know, Mom."

"Then how can you even think of another man? It seems like, well, like a—sin."

"A sin?"

"Yes."

Lexie brought to mind each verse of Scripture she could recall concerning marriage. "I don't know of any admonition in the Bible that forbids widows to remarry."

"I can't say that I do, either." She shuddered. "I'm still not sure it's right for you even to be thinking about it." She placed her hand on Lexie's shoulder. "I know things are tough for you right now and that you haven't recovered from the expenses. I wish your father and I were in a better position ourselves, so we could offer you more help. Maybe I could talk to him—"

"No, that's okay. The reason I moved in the first place was to gain more independence."

"I know, but I don't think that means you should strike up a romance with the first old friend you run into."

"Theo just did me a favor, Mom. Kassia said she would have brought me if she hadn't needed to go in to her office tomorrow."

"On a Saturday?"

"She's dedicated to her job. You have to be nowadays."

"I suppose so. I'm not sure the changes the world has seen since I was a young woman have been for the better."

"There's not much we can do about it." Lexie shrugged and smiled at her mother, grateful she'd been distracted by another subject.

"Take your father's mother, for instance," Mom continued. "She lost her husband in World War II, leaving her alone to raise your father and your two aunts by herself. And she never remarried. She stuck it out and did a fine job with all her kids."

Lexie nodded at the familiar story. As much as she admired her grandmother, she wanted to be her own person instead of patterning her life after someone else's. But arguing with her mother wouldn't help. "I know, Mom. And I know you want what's best for Piper and me. I promise I'll keep the whole situation in prayer."

"That's a good idea."

Lexie wished she could forget her mother's guilt inducing words about Curt, but she knew it was impossible. She had to think of her daughter now. And of Theo.

"Do you have everything?" Theo asked as Lexie approached.

"Enough to see me through the night."

"I'll be back tomorrow morning, if you like."

"Yes, that would be nice."

"I told Theo he could spend the night with us," Dad said, "but he had already reserved a hotel room."

"I knew you'd offer. I tried to keep him from calling ahead in the car, but he wouldn't listen," Lexie explained. But she understood Theo's—and her parents'—need to be alone after such a stressful evening.

"Maybe next time. I appreciate the offer all the same," Theo said.

"Good night. See you in the morning."

Lexie wasn't surprised when Theo gave her a longing look, but she was both surprised and pleased when he gave Piper a similar look of warmth and concern. She was just as delighted when her daughter smiled back.

Could Theo love Piper already?

eleven

Lexie made herself a temporary bed out of a chair and hospital linens. Just to sleep beside Piper was worth the discomfort.

"Mommy?"

"Yes?"

"Is Theo like Mr. Mathis?"

Lexie searched her mind and decided Piper must have been referring to the dad of a friend from preschool. "Mr. Mathis? You mean, Jessica's father?"

"Uh huh."

"What do you mean?"

"Well, one day her real dad just left, and then her mommy got married to somebody else."

"Are you afraid of that? That I might marry someone else?"

"I don't know." She shrugged. "I guess not, if he's nice. Is Theo nice, Mommy?"

Lexie stroked her daughter's hair. "I think he's nice. He's just my friend, though."

"Oh." The smile disappeared from her face.

Lexie swallowed. Surely Piper wanted a father in her life. Maybe more than Lexie realized. "You don't need to worry about anything right now. It's just you and me tonight. I want you to get some sleep so you can leave the hospital bright and early tomorrow, okay?"

Piper yawned. "Okay."

The last sound she heard was the EKG monitor beeping at regular intervals. With Piper by her side, Lexie slept more soundly than she expected. More soundly than she had in a long time.

2a

"I think she'll be fine," the doctor informed Lexie the next morning after unhooking Piper from the monitor. "We didn't see any irregularities in her heartbeat or any other abnormalities. She can go home today."

Lexie sighed with relief. "Thank you."

"Can I get out of bed now?" Piper asked.

"You sure can," the doctor said. "Mrs. Zoltan, since you've learned your daughter likes to raid the medicine cabinet, you need to be more careful with how you store medications."

Lexie fought the urge to defend herself and her mother. "I know. I don't think this will be happening again."

"Let's hope not." The doctor turned her attention to Piper. "You won't be eating any more pills without an adult saying it's okay, will you?"

"No!"

"I think we've all learned our lesson," Lexie agreed.

"Good. Just keep a close watch on her for the next few days, and call me if you have any concerns."

Piper was dressed in a pair of black jeans and a T-shirt when Theo entered a few minutes later. "Everybody sleep well?"

"Better than ever," Lexie answered. With the scare of Piper's visit to the hospital behind them, seeing Theo made her feel even more reassured.

"Hi, Mr. Powers," Piper greeted him.

"Hey, there!" Theo waved. "I brought you a present." He handed her a bag decorated with a picture of Winnie the Pooh. A rectangular box peeked out from underneath yellow tissue paper.

Piper squealed and clapped her hands, then reached for the box. "I know what this is, Mr. Powers. It's a doll."

"Well, you'll just have to see."

Piper tore through the paper in a flash. She drew in her breath when she saw the blue eyed blond doll wearing a long blue dress. "She's pretty! She can go home and live with all my other dolls. I think they'll like her." Piper brought the doll up to her neck and embraced it, swaying back and forth.

"Watch out, or she'll smother in your hair," Lexie cautioned.

"Oh!" Piper released her embrace and started to walk the doll, although the result looked more like hopping. She held up the doll for her new bear to see. "What do you think, Peanut Butter? Do you like her?" Piper moved the bear's head up and down. "She likes her!"

"Good!" Theo said amid Lexie's chuckles. "I wasn't sure what to get you. I just have nephews."

"What's nephews?"

"He's an uncle to boys," Lexie explained.

"Boys!" Piper scrunched her nose. "Yuck. I don't like boys."

"You will one day," Lexie said laughing, then turned to Theo. "You didn't have to bring her anything, but she surely does like the doll you picked out." Lexie tapped Piper on the shoulder. "What do you say, Piper?"

"Umm." Piper's eyes looked upward.

"The magic word."

"Please?"

"No."

"Oh. Thank you, Mr. Powers."

"You're welcome," he answered.

"As you can see, we're still polishing our manners," Lexie apologized.

"I think she's doing very well. But if you don't mind, can she call me Theo? I feel so old with her calling me Mr. Powers. Not that I want to undermine what you're trying to teach her," he added quickly.

"That's all right. Part of etiquette is making the other person comfortable. She can call you Theo if you like."

"She seems to know how to respect her elders. Don't you, Piper?"

"Sure do!" She twisted her mouth. "Hey, does this present and me callin' you Theo and stuff mean you're my new daddy?"

"Piper!" Lexie's cheeks warmed. "What—what made you think such a thing?"

She shrugged. "Grammy was saying stuff."

Lexie groaned. "Kids overhear—and misinterpret—everything," she said to Theo.

"That's okay. I guess it's only natural for her to want a father." Theo's calm words didn't match the nervous way he drummed his fingers on the table that held the breakfast tray.

Lexie looked at her daughter. "As I explained to you before, Mr. Powers—I mean, Theo—is just a good friend of Mommy's."

"Oh." The corners of Piper's mouth tilted downward. She stared at the doll so that Lexie could only see her long eyelashes.

Lexie wondered why Piper seemed so disappointed. Sure, Theo had brought her a gift, but she already owned plenty of dolls. And of course he was handsome and kind to her and apparently liked her. But Lexie couldn't believe Piper wanted Theo to take Curt's place. Not that she remembered Curt. Still, most of the other children at Piper's preschool had daddies. Wouldn't it be normal for Piper to wish she had a daddy, too?

No, she couldn't be so captivated with Theo himself. Like any little girl, Piper's romantic fantasies carried her into a world of ease and fun. The idea of having a daddy—any daddy—played a role in the little girl's dreams. Theo embodied the idea. That's all.

Just make sure you don't fall in love with the idea yourself—or with the thought of having a husband again. If you do, you'll be on dangerous ground.

≈

That afternoon at the Downeys' house, Theo tried not to

look too enthusiastic about the thick steak Lexie's dad had grilled. With the outer layer cooked to a deep brown and the inside warm and pink, Theo could hardly wait to savor a big chunk.

"So do you think you'll be going back to work this week?" Mrs. Downey asked.

"I haven't decided yet." He wondered if her question was a hint that she hoped he'd be leaving soon.

"I think he's going to wait for me to go back," Lexie said.

"That's awfully nice of you, Theo, but we can take Lexie back to Richmond ourselves," said Mrs. Downey. "Assuming she hasn't changed her mind about living so far away from home."

Theo's throat tightened. Had Lexie changed her mind? Did she plan to stay in North Carolina? His deep disappointment at the possibility surprised him, even though he knew he had strong feelings for her.

Lord, I haven't felt this way since Lexie and I were in college together. Should I follow my heart? I want to follow Your will, though, not my own.

Lexie's sweet voice broke into his silent petition. "I'm glad you want me to be home, Mom, but I think I'll stay. I really like my work, as I told you before."

"That's what you say now," she muttered.

Theo wondered what Mrs. Downey meant. He glanced at Lexie, but she had become absorbed in finishing her tossed salad.

"Theo, you've gone to enough trouble," Mr. Downey interjected.

"I do appreciate everything you've done," Lexie added, finally looking at him.

"But we understand," Lexie's mother said, "if you have to leave."

"You're not leavin', are you, Theo?" Piper asked. "You

promised you'd look at my rock collection."

"Of course I'll look at your rock collection. I wouldn't dream of leaving before I see that!" Theo assured her.

Piper pushed back her chair. "Let's go now. It's in my room."

"Not yet, young lady," Lexie said gently. She pointed to Piper's plate, which still had salad and carrots on it.

The little girl shifted in her seat. "But I don't wanna eat that stuff. I don't like vegetables."

"I know you don't, but you have to get some nutrition. You can't live on cookies and ice cream."

"But I ate my hot dog."

"I know. But at least finish your salad, okay?"

Piper nodded but with a frown.

"I hope you didn't want me to see your rock collection so you could get out of eating your vegetables," Theo teased.

The other adults laughed. Even Mrs. Downey chuckled.

"What's so funny?" Piper asked.

"You'll understand some day," Lexie said.

After dinner Theo helped clear the dishes.

"If you think this will get you on my good side, you're right." Mrs. Downey smiled.

Theo felt someone tugging on his free hand.

"Will you come and look at my rocks now?" Piper asked, smiling up at him. "See this!" She held up a stone angled into the letter *L*. "I found it in the backyard yesterday. Pops said we should try to find the whole alphabet. I already found *D* and *T*. Wanna see?"

"Sure, as long as I'm finished here in the kitchen."

Lexie hung the dishtowel on a rack. "You're done." She smiled and nodded toward a hallway just off the kitchen. "Let's go."

"Race ya!" Piper squealed.

"Okay, Honey! Are you in, Theo?" Lexie grinned.

He had no idea how two adults and one child could race

through the narrow hall. "Um, sure."

They lined up; then Piper stretched out her arms, holding the adults back. "On your mark. Get set." Piper started running. "Go!"

Piper laughed as she set off. Lexie followed closely behind, with Theo coming in a distant third. Piper ran into her room and over to the bed, hopping on top of the covers.

She knelt on the bed and extended her arms toward the ceiling. "I win!"

"I don't know about that, young lady. You held us back and started before you said 'go'." Lexie shook her finger in mock chastisement.

Piper giggled. "I still won."

"I don't know, either." Theo shook his head, his eyes twinkling. "I think your mom's right."

"I don't care. I win anyway." Piper's laughter filled the room. She leapt off the bed and bounded toward a small white dresser with pink handles. Among a menagerie of miniature toys and trinkets, Piper found a cardboard box. She opened it, peered inside, and extracted two rocks.

"Look!" She held them up for Theo to see.

"I see!"

She showed him a jagged gray rock. "See, this one looks like a *D*."

Theo studied the rock, trying to figure out how she could conclude it resembled the letter. Using his vivid imagination he thought he could see the possibilities. "Uh-huh! How about that?"

"And look at this one. I found it in the parkin' lot of the grocery store yesterday. It looks just like a *T*."

Theo nodded. This rock looked more like the letter Piper suggested. "I see. Good job!"

"How long do you think it will take to find the whole alphabet?"

"All twenty-six letters?" Theo rubbed his chin as if in deep contemplation.

"How many is twenty-six?"

"A lot!" Lexie exclaimed. "I think it will take you at least a month to find that many, and at that pace you'd be finding a new letter almost every day."

"A month?" Piper asked. "How long is that? Till Christmas?"

"Oh, it's several months before Christmas," Lexie told her.

"Oh." Piper frowned. "That's a long time."

"It's not even cold yet," Theo said. "We have the rest of the summer, and then the leaves have to turn red and orange in the fall. Then there's Thanksgiving. And only after that can you have Christmas."

"That's forever!" Piper said.

"It will be here sooner than you think," Lexie said. "You'll be having a birthday before Christmas comes."

"Not until after Turkey Day," Piper said.

Theo and Lexie looked at each other and laughed.

"It's not funny! That's a long time."

"But you can pass the time by finding all your rocks," Theo pointed out. "A lot of the letters will be hard."

"Which ones?"

"Oh, like *Q* and *S* and *W*. But you'll find every letter before you know it. Maybe I can help you."

Maybe I can help you? Why did I say that?

Theo kicked himself mentally for suggesting something he might not be able to follow through on. He never wanted to hurt the child by making a promise he couldn't keep.

He watched Lexie stroke Piper's hair. In college he thought she was nearly perfect. He never expected to find her even more appealing in her role as a mother. But he did.

He wanted to stay. He never wanted to leave. But he had to.

"We can look all day tomorrow," Lexie said.

Her words consoled him. Looking for rocks tomorrow

would be in keeping with his promise. Theo held back an audible sigh of relief.

"That'll be fun," he said aloud.

Assured they would hunt for rocks the next day, Piper asked Lexie to read her a bedtime story.

"I'll leave you two alone," Theo said. "See you tomorrow."

"I guess you'll have to go back on Monday," Lexie said quietly.

"I'm going to call in on Monday morning. I'd like to take a few days off. We happen to have a lag in work at the office now, and I have the time coming to me."

"Really? You're gonna stay?" Piper clapped her hands.

Lexie's face lit up. "Are you sure it's okay? I don't want to cause you to run into trouble with your boss."

An image of Ms. Thorndike, his supervisor, popped into his head. Theo couldn't envision her as a mother, though pictures of four children adorned her desk. She carried out her role at the office in a tough manner, but she appreciated Theo's work. The government had been facing lean times recently. As one of the younger employees, Theo made sure he didn't gripe or complain about taking on more work to make up for those who had retired or moved on, whose positions were left unfilled indefinitely.

Since he hadn't taken a vacation in over a year, he didn't think it would be a problem to have a few days off. Besides, the situation had developed into a life altering event—for all of them. If he ever planned to renew his relationship with Lexie and get to know her little girl, he couldn't dawdle. He was certain his reluctance to speak up, to express his feelings to Lexie, had contributed to his losing her in college.

Theo shrugged. "She's cool. She knows I work hard. She'll approve a few days of leave for me so I can stay awhile."

Lexie spoke just above a whisper. "That would be wonderful."

❧

By the following Friday, Theo felt as though the Downeys' place was his second home. Even Lexie's mom didn't seem to mind his presence.

Each day had passed quickly, filled with fun activities. Piper's preschool had already let out for the summer, so they had no particular schedule to keep. Instead they found something new to do each day.

"I don't know when the last time was I went to the zoo," Lexie told Theo as they left nearby Asheboro. "We always lived so close, but I never seemed to find the time."

"That's what they say. The people who live near the tourist attractions never seem to visit them. Most of the people I know who live in Richmond haven't seen the Edgar Allan Poe, Valentine, or Confederate museums."

"Museums. Yuck. They're boring," Piper said, hanging on to her mother's hand.

Lexie chuckled.

"Museums have pretty pictures," Theo said.

"I don't care. I'd rather go to the park."

Theo tousled Piper's hair. "You did that, too."

"Yeah!" She looked up at him. "Can we go back today?"

"Hmm." Lexie smiled. "I see she's asking you and not me. She's already found out you're a soft touch."

"What's a soft touch?" Piper asked.

"It means he lets you have your way," Lexie explained.

"He doesn't always let me have my way. He didn't take us to the toy store yesterday."

"I guess you're right," Lexie observed. "You had just been to the store the day before."

"But I like to go every day!"

"It's a good thing we have to go back tomorrow," Lexie told Theo. "Otherwise we'd all be broke."

"So can we go to the park now?"

Lexie looked at her watch. "I wish we could, but it's getting too late. You need to be in bed before long."

"Aww! But I don't want to! Can't I stay up?"

"Not tonight, unless Grammy says it's okay. You'll be staying with her for a little while."

Piper stopped. "You mean you're leavin' again?"

&

She hadn't anticipated telling Piper about her plans while they were still in the parking lot, but she knew her daughter wouldn't be put off. Lexie bent down in front of her child. She kept her voice low. "Yes, but this time I want you to go with me. Would that be okay?"

"Can Grammy and Pops go, too?"

"I wish they could, but they have to stay here. Pops has to go to work."

"Oh. I wish there wasn't any work."

"I know." Lexie rubbed her palms against Piper's forearms, a gesture that always seemed to calm them both. "So you want to come with me, don't you?"

Piper nodded.

"Good!" Lexie spread out her arms, and Piper rushed into them. They held each other tightly.

Lexie stood and motioned to Theo. He had been walking around in slow circles, studying the trees and the other cars in the lot. She wondered how much of their conversation he'd heard.

Theo had been the picture of amiability during their time together. He seemed to slide naturally into a role of caring for Piper. Yet the setting was idyllic. No work or school responsibilities hindered their time together. Each day was free, a gift to do with as they would. In reality every day couldn't be filled with trips to the zoo, informal dates with Theo, or visits to the toy store. How was Theo feeling? Was he as fond of Piper as he appeared to be? Or was he just being the nice gentleman he always was, showing them a good time since Piper's life had been endangered? Did she dare let herself fall in love with Theo?

Lexie wished she could hold on to these days forever and never have to return to her new home or her job or to finding day care for Piper or confronting the mound of debt that awaited.

But she couldn't. It was time to grow up. Time to take full responsibility for her little girl.

She only hoped Theo would be there, too.

twelve

Theo tried to concentrate on lifting weights but kept losing count during each set of repetitions. Ever since he had driven Lexie and Piper to Richmond, his thoughts were never far from them. He tried calling several times, only to reach Kassia's answering machine. Perhaps that was best. They needed time to settle into their new lives.

He sat up on the weight bench and wiped his face with his hand towel. Never did he think he would love a child, especially one that didn't bear his last name, as he loved Piper. Surely Lexie could see he adored her and would be a good father to her. But something was holding Lexie back. His own selfishness perhaps? Why wouldn't Lexie think him selfish? He had done nothing but talk about a life without children since they reunited—an extension of the feelings he had expressed all through school. Why would she think bringing Piper presents and taking the two of them on day trips for a week would change anything?

Lord, do You want me to be a father to Piper? And if that is Your will, how can I convince Lexie I'm worthy of her? Or of Piper?

❦

A week had passed since Lexie and Piper had settled into Kassia's apartment. Although the days weren't as idyllic as they had been with Theo, Lexie felt cheered to have Piper with her. She'd been able to place her in a reliable day-care situation, and the evenings, for the most part, belonged to the two of them.

At the same time she missed Theo. With the adjustments of three people living in an apartment meant for one, Lexie had managed only to leave a message on his phone. She resolved to cook a nice dinner for him soon. That was the least she could do.

But now a stack of mail awaited on the desk in the bedroom. She had put off looking through it, knowing she would only feel discouraged. She sorted through the junk, throwing out catalogs that might tempt her to buy items she couldn't afford. Even the ones that offered inexpensive dresses, sometimes with the mom's dress to match, or the ones that screamed "Summer Sale" in red letters.

She sighed. She had never been one to spend money with abandon, but she wished she could at least buy a few little luxuries. If only she could pick up a pretty dress for Piper without worrying about her tight budget. Even when Curt was living, finances had been lean. Now that he was gone. . .

Lexie held back her tears. The catalogs had been trying enough. She was in no mood to tackle the stack of bills.

Piper chose that moment to burst into the room they shared. "What's wrong, Mommy?"

Lexie wiped away a stray tear and swivelled in her chair. "It's okay, Honey. Mommy had something in her eye."

I did have something in my eye. A tear.

"Oh." Piper yanked a tissue out of the box on Lexie's desk and handed it to her mother. "Here you go."

"Thanks." Lexie accepted the tissue and swiped at her eyes and nose. "What are you up to now?"

Piper shrugged. "I dunno. Miss Kassia said to come in here with you 'cause there's something on the TV that wouldn't be good for me to see."

Lexie glanced at the clock. "It's eight o'clock and time for you to go to bed anyway."

"Aww! I knew you'd say that. Can't I help you instead?"

"Maybe someday, when you're old enough to write."

"I never get any mail."

"Grammy writes every week."

"But that's all I ever get. I wish I got as much mail as you do."

"No, you don't." Lexie smiled. "Now come on—let's get you into bed."

Since the room was small, Lexie and Piper shared a bed. Lexie worried that Piper might grow too accustomed to such an arrangement, but the situation couldn't be helped. Kassia's couch wasn't available since she spent most evenings in front of the television. Lexie didn't care to toss and turn on the uncomfortable cushions after Kassia turned in, which was usually past midnight.

Brad had been scarce since that one night he had come to the apartment. Lexie supposed Kassia's mindless television viewing was better than her spending her evenings with Brad. Kassia surely didn't need him in her life. Although she hadn't complained about Lexie's new roommate, the atmosphere around the apartment had changed after Piper's arrival. Before, Kassia and Lexie could more or less come and go as they pleased. If they chose to eat out together or even double date, they could.

Holding back a sigh, Lexie determined to find a better place soon—when she could round up enough money for a deposit and budget for a full month's rent.

Piper had barely said "amen" after her evening prayer when she pulled on the cuff of Lexie's blouse. "Can you stay here and go to sleep with me?"

"Not quite yet. I'll be back soon." Lexie grabbed Peanut Butter from the top of the bedside table. The bear had never been far out of reach since Piper's hospital stay. Lexie handed the toy to her daughter. "Peanut Butter will keep you company until I get back."

"I guess." The little girl frowned. "Can you stay home tomorrow? I don't want to go back to the center. I don't have any friends there."

"I know it's hard at first since you're new. But you'll make friends soon. And just think—you'll go to kindergarten next year. You'll make lots of new friends there."

Before Piper could argue, Kassia called to Lexie. "Telephone!"

Lexie had been so engrossed in putting Piper to bed that she hadn't heard the phone ring. "Okay."

"Who is it?" Piper asked.

"Well, Grammy called yesterday, so it's probably just someone wanting Mommy to buy something. I'll have to find out. Now you go to sleep—okay?"

Piper nodded.

Lexie wasn't eager to take the call. Lately she had lagged behind on a department store credit card bill, which resulted in interest plus late fees, increasing the debt even more. So much for trying to save a few dollars at a sale. She wished she hadn't accepted the store's offer of ten percent off for their credit card. She remembered the promotional gift—a water bottle—that sweetened the deal. She'd taken the bottle with her on two jogs before the straw broke, leaving it useless. Though the gift was long gone, credit card bills arrived at brutally regular intervals. The store had already called once. She hoped it wasn't them again. Kassia was sure to be upset if bill collectors made a habit of calling the apartment.

"Hello?" she asked hesitantly.

"Hi, Lexie. It's Theo."

She let out her breath. "Oh, good."

"I'm glad it's good to hear from me, but that's a funny greeting. Were you expecting bad news?"

"Uh, not really. I don't know." *So much for wit.*

"I saw an apartment for rent near my house. I was wondering if you'd like to look at it."

"Near your house, eh?" She smiled into the phone. "Do I sense an ulterior motive?" *I hope.*

"Who, me? Ulterior motive? I've never heard of such a

thing." He chuckled. "Okay, I guess I'd like to know you're not having to bunk up with a roommate anymore. And I know this is a good neighborhood. But even though it's nearer to me, I promise not to pester you."

Lexie laughed. "You never pester us. Piper has been asking about you. She misses you." *And so do I.*

"Tell her I miss her, too," Theo said. "It's been crazy at work since I missed so much time. I've had to catch up."

"Sorry."

"Don't be. So would you like to take a look at the apartment? Maybe tomorrow? I can go with you if you like."

"So we'll look like a family—a reliable bunch?"

"I was thinking more that you might want another opinion. I bought this house by myself, and I would have liked having a little moral support."

"How can I pass up such a good offer? Okay. I'll meet you after work."

❧

Lexie turned the key and opened the door to the vacant unit. The landlord had given it to Theo and Lexie so they could view the apartment by themselves.

As Lexie stepped across the threshold, Theo imagined her coming in from a hard day at the office to her own place. He entered behind her.

The small room had bare, off-white walls and a beige carpet. Off to one side, on a patch of beige vinyl flooring, was a kitchen. Directly opposite, beige floor length curtains hung in front of sliding glass doors. Beside the kitchen, a hallway led to the rest of the apartment, which the landlord said contained two bedrooms, a powder room, and a full bathroom.

"I love it already!" Lexie lifted her hands to the sky and twirled around the vacant room.

"Really?"

Lexie rushed to the kitchen area and opened the microwave.

"Wow! It has a rotating dish. Even Kassia's doesn't have that." She peered into the dishwasher. "Looks almost new. No rusted spindles or anything."

"Great." He tried to remember all the details the landlord had mentioned. One negative item came to mind. "I just wish each unit had a washer and dryer for you. That would be so much better than having to do your laundry in the next building."

"Yes, but I can manage."

Theo surveyed the area with a more critical look. "Of course, most places you find will have a dull beige carpet and lackluster color on the walls." The area seemed so small. By the time she'd moved in furniture, it was bound to seem even smaller. "This is where you'll be doing most of your living, and it isn't nearly as big as Kassia's apartment. The kitchen opens into the living area, and you won't have a dining room."

"I don't care. I'm just happy to find a place this reasonable where I can feel that Piper is safe." She turned her face toward the sliding glass door. "And look. A balcony." She motioned for him to join her. "Come on."

She drew the curtain to one side, then walked out onto a small slab of concrete surrounded by black metal bars that reminded Theo of a prison.

To his surprise Lexie was still smiling when he joined her. He tapped the top of the bars. "Gorgeous, huh? Early Alcatraz?"

"Maybe so." She patted the bars, which were no farther apart than the width of her hand. "I can tell this is good enough to keep Piper safe out here, especially since we're just on the second level. Her safety is the most important thing."

"That's true," Theo said, nodding.

Lexie pointed to the corner. "I think this is wide enough for me to put a couple of patio chairs here."

"You may be right." He leaned on the railing. "Beautiful view of the parking lot."

"I always did like cars."

He couldn't help but laugh. "You're determined not to find a thing wrong with this place, aren't you?"

She laughed. "Well, let me look in the bedrooms."

"Okay. I'll stay out here."

"Are you sure?"

Theo nodded. Perhaps if Lexie could have a few moments alone, she could look at the place objectively. At least she hadn't brought Piper. A child's emotional response to a new place would be far more compelling than any other factor. Lexie needed a clear head if she was going to commit to an apartment for a year.

"I'll be right back."

Theo watched the people who might soon be Lexie's neighbors as they came and went. When he'd first learned about the vacant apartment, he had made sure the complex welcomed children. A well maintained playground awaited Piper upon her arrival. Not many children were playing there when he'd come, but the day was hot. Theo just hoped Piper would soon make friends.

And Lexie?

A lump formed in his throat. A feeling he didn't like. Lexie was still young. She was sure to meet plenty of men, maybe even single fathers with children similar in age and temperament to Piper.

What is wrong with you? Don't you want her to be happy?

Yes, but not with someone else.

The declaration from his conscience no longer surprised him. Old and new feelings had stirred during their time together. He had given her some space when they returned home. Too much space, maybe. When she hadn't called, he'd found an excuse—this apartment—to contact her.

He drummed his fingers absently on the railing. His first thought was how ugly it looked. Lexie's first thought was how it would be safe for her daughter.

Sure, I love Piper. Who wouldn't? But am I ready to take on a woman with a child? I feel like a child half the time myself.

The doubt that clouded his mind felt worse than the lump in his stomach. He didn't want to think about anything now, at least not anything except making Lexie happy.

He heard the sliding door moving on its track. "So what did you think?" he asked, turning to Lexie.

"I can't believe how large my room is. It has a walk-in closet!" Lexie's face was flushed and her voice excited. "Piper's room is a little smaller, but it's plenty big for her needs. Much larger than the room she has at Mom and Dad's."

"Great! Then you're all set."

"I think so. I'm a little nervous about signing my life away on the lease." She rushed back through the sliding glass doors and into the living room.

Theo followed her inside. "You can afford this place, can't you? I mean, if it's okay for me to ask. If you don't want to tell me, that's fine. I understand. I know you haven't been on your new job long, and you've had a lot of expense. But even if the rent is absolutely no problem, don't think you have to take this place because I mentioned it. This surely isn't the only complex in town." He knew he sounded like a babbling idiot. He was talking and couldn't stop. "Trust me—I won't be offended if you decide to walk out the door this instant and never look back."

"Whoa! It seems you're having buyer's remorse instead of me." She placed her hands on her hips and cocked her head. "What is it? I know. You don't want me to blame you if this turns out to be a big mistake. That must be why you've had nothing but bad things to say about this apartment from the moment we walked in."

Theo thought for a moment. "You know, maybe that's it. I just didn't realize it."

"Well, you don't have to worry. I appreciate your going to all the trouble to find this place for me and now coming out here with me to check it out." She held up three fingers. "Girl Scout's honor, I promise I won't blame you if the toilet leaks or the stove doesn't work or if the neighbors argue all night."

He shuddered. "Don't even suggest such a thing. It might turn out to be a self-fulfilling prophecy." He looked toward the bathroom. "And come to think of it, you'd probably better flush the toilets and turn on the appliances, just in case."

"Oh, I'm sure everything works fine." She opened each cabinet door and looked inside as though she were a small child with her first dollhouse.

"You have fun here then. I'll go check out everything for you."

"Don't worry about it." She turned toward him and took his hands in hers. Their warmth sent a pleasant wave through him.

"I really appreciate everything you've done for Piper and me. You've gone way beyond the call of friendship. I don't know what I would have done without you."

He moved closer and put his arms around her. Though small, Lexie's body had just enough flesh on her bones so she felt soft. He wanted to kiss her, more than he ever had, a feeling he hadn't thought possible after the night at the restaurant. Theo hoped she felt the same. He lowered his face toward hers.

Suddenly she pulled away. "Theo."

"What?" He stepped back.

"I'm sorry." She folded her arms and stared at the carpet. "It's my fault."

"What do you mean, it's your fault? I don't see anything wrong here. Aren't you happy?"

She nodded but clasped her arms more tightly around herself. "I like you. I like you a lot. But we can never be more than friends."

Why didn't she simply take a knife and lance his heart? "Okay, maybe I've been too pushy. Maybe I should have given you more space. But you don't have to give me that 'let's just be friends' line."

"It's not a line. I wish things could be different."

"But they can be."

"No, they can't." She sighed. "Look—you've been wonderful to Piper. I couldn't have asked for anyone nicer. But I also know what's important to you. You've already made it clear to me time and time again that you don't want a family. You even said you weren't sure if you wanted children at all."

"But what about the time we spent together?"

"That wasn't reality. Life is not an endless stream of free time to visit zoos and museums and have picnics," she said. "Life is getting someone else ready for day care and going to work. Then rushing out of the office to be sure Piper is picked up in time so there's no extra charge. Along with those things is the guilt I feel because I'm not doing enough at work—or at home, either. Then there're the bills. I shop at consignment and thrift stores trying to keep us looking decent, and I buy everything I can on sale. Piper gets a little Social Security check every month since Curt died, and that helps. But most of the time there is more month than money at our house."

Theo glanced around the apartment. "Maybe I shouldn't have mentioned this place."

"No. Don't think that. I'm glad you did. I have to leave Kassia's place. She's a lot like you. She wants to live the single life, to have adventure, to come and go as she pleases. Look at the situation with Brad. It was bad enough when I was the only one there; but now that Piper has joined us, I'm sure I'm cramping her style."

"I don't know about Kassia, but who said you were cramping my style? I want you in my life, but not just as a friend." As soon as the words left his mouth, he felt a mixture of relief, anticipation, regret, and angst.

Lexie looked down at the carpet for a moment.

"You say that now," she finally answered, "but no one understands the reality of raising a child unless they've done it."

"Piper is a sweet little girl. She'll be a breeze to raise, I'm sure. And what we don't know, we can learn together."

"I doubt if any child is a breeze to raise, although I have to admit Piper is pretty special," Lexie said. "But being a parent isn't the same. We can't expect to take her climbing up the Swiss Alps during the school year or parasailing in the Caribbean." She returned her gaze to the floor. "You have a right to find someone else, someone who is free to go with you, without a child, at least at the start. Then when you've had your adventures, you can have your own family together."

"So I have no say in this at all? You've made this decision based on a perception of me you formed during college?"

"No, I've made it for all of us." She blinked, her eyes moist. "We'll only hold you back. You need to pursue your dreams. Dreams you've held for a long time. If you don't, you'll only resent both of us."

"No, I won't."

"I think you will. Come on—let's go. I have to sign the papers, and I promised Kassia I wouldn't leave her with Piper too long." She retrieved her bag from the top of the stove and headed out the door before he could say another word.

Theo could see he had no choice but to follow her. If only he could make a good argument. But he knew in his heart that she spoke some truth. His life was still stuck in the post-college style. He had a house, but he occupied it like an apartment. It was temporary. "Committed" was not a word he would use to describe his life now.

I must change my life, Lord. Please guide me, he prayed.

thirteen

Several weeks later Lexie was filling out a new form at work when she glimpsed Darren sauntering over to her. She hunched her shoulders over the document and stared at it in hopes he would take the hint. Since Lexie's first day on the job, Darren often stopped by her desk on some pretext. Her chilly civility, rather than turning him off, attracted him even more. Just like the authors of *The Rules* promised. If only they hadn't been right!

Ignoring her concentration, Darren leaned over her desk. "So how about a day at King's Dominion? This Saturday. It'll be fun."

Even though Lexie had been expecting Darren to ask her out for some time, she was still taken aback by his abruptness. "You get right to the point, don't you?"

"No reason not to. You never get what you don't ask for. Isn't that right?" He took a sip of coffee from his mug.

"I suppose so."

Darren seemed pleasant enough, and riding roller coasters and seeing shows would be a nice diversion. Maybe enough to keep her mind off Theo for a day.

But the diversion would come at a price. She would either have to ask Kassia to sacrifice a Saturday or come up with money she didn't have for a babysitter she hardly knew. She didn't dare ask Darren if she could bring her four year old, which would mean they'd have to spend the day in the children's section.

She looked at her desk calendar. Piper was supposed to be at a birthday party at three o'clock. Asking someone else to take her, or asking Piper to miss it, would be out of the question.

She shook her head. "I don't think so, but thanks."

"I won't make you ride the roller coasters if you don't want to."

"I know." She smiled. Darren and she were equals, so she knew her job wasn't on the line if she didn't accept. Still, she sensed he wasn't a man who took rejection well. "I'd really like to go, but my little girl has something going on just about every weekend."

He studied the photos on her desk. "Oh. That's your little girl? I never pictured you as a mom. I thought she was your niece or something."

"Well, I'm a mom—and proud of it." She picked up the most recent photo, a snapshot of Piper hugging Peanut Butter. Every time she saw the picture, she was reminded of Theo. She handed it to Darren so he could take a closer look.

"Yeah. She's cute," he said in a flat voice and returned the photo.

Lexie replaced it on her desk. She couldn't help but compare Darren's offhanded remark to the way Theo's eyes lit up when he saw Piper.

"I don't mind that. I'm divorced myself. My ex has custody of our boys. I didn't know you were divorced, too. I'll bet you're a lot nicer about child support than my ex." He gritted his teeth and rolled his eyes. "Ashleigh—that's my ex—she's constantly harassing me. I do the best I can, but she doesn't seem to understand."

"I'm sure you do. I don't have any of those issues, though."

"Oh." An embarrassed look crossed his face. "You're just a single parent? That takes some courage."

"I had a husband at one time. He went home to the Lord a couple of years ago."

"He went where?"

Lexie tightened her lips. "He died." She wished she could keep the unpleasant tone out of her voice.

"Oh. I thought you said he went home. Sorry." He drummed his fingers against the side of the partition. "So I guess it's okay for you to see other people now?"

"Yes."

"So how about Sunday? We can be there when the park opens."

"We try to go to church on Sundays."

A blank expression crossed his face. "Can't you skip one Sunday?"

"I don't like to. Besides, Piper—that's my little girl—enjoys Sunday school."

He stepped back. "Too bad. You can go to church any time, but I don't have every weekend open."

How am I to respond? Thank you for making time in your busy schedule to ask me out? How arrogant can you get?

Feeling that almost anything she could say would be wrong, Lexie simply smiled and turned away to concentrate on one of the many forms she needed to complete before the end of the month.

Darren left her desk quickly enough. Lexie tried to think about her work, but focusing on paperwork was difficult when all she could think about was what Darren could be telling the rest of the office about her. Maybe she should tell everyone she made it a policy not to date anyone at work. But that might fuel the gossip mill even more.

She stared at the form but saw only lines. Was her mother right? Was she betraying Curt even to be thinking about other men? Then again, Mom had warmed up to Theo during their time together.

I don't know what to think. I'm so confused.

She glanced at Darren's workstation situated on the other side of the maze of desks. He was away, probably telling his friends how snobby she was. For the hundredth time she noticed on the wall near his desk a poster of an attractive model running along the beach, a revealing bikini advertising—what? The suit? The beach? The model? She didn't want to know.

Shuddering, Lexie realized that, as attractive as Darren appeared, he had offered little to cause her to want to be with him.

But Theo did.

Ever since she'd rebuffed Theo at the apartment a few weeks ago, her heart felt as though it were leaking out a little bit of love each day, love that only he could capture and refill. But she couldn't let him.

He had wanted to kiss her. She knew it. She had wanted that kiss as well, maybe even more than he had. But she had turned him away. The hurt look in his eyes made her wish things could be different. Sure, she gave him the standard excuses—the ones that made it seem as if she were thinking only of Theo and his need for adventure. And she was. Up to a point. But she didn't want Theo to resent Piper and her. He didn't need to be tied down to her financial debt nor watch years pass before he could go on the exotic adventures he so wanted. But her own guilt—the constant guilt her mother had placed in her mind over being unfaithful to Curt—was a factor as well.

Father in heaven, am I making a mistake? Maybe the biggest mistake of my life—?

Jennifer tapped on her shoulder, startling her from her thoughts. "I hear you shot down Darren." She grinned.

Lexie moaned. "So he's already told everybody in the office?"

"He didn't tell me. Cindy did."

The biggest gossip in the office. That was just great. "What's he saying about me?"

"Who knows? Who cares? Nobody will believe him anyway. All I can say is, good for you. Ever since he got divorced, he thinks every woman in the office wants him. He'll know better now." She rapped her pen against the top of Lexie's desk. "And so will the other guys. Let's see—first you threw Theo out of your apartment. That reminds me—when are you going to set us up?"

Lexie held back a groan. Even though Theo wasn't hers, she hardly wanted to arrange a match between him and someone else.

She was thankful Jennifer was enjoying the conversation too much to dwell on the question. "So first it was Theo, now Darren. How many men does this make now that you've turned down since you got here?"

Lexie counted four in her mind, including Darren. That made almost every single man under the age of forty in the office. Modesty precluded her from giving Jennifer an exact count, so she simply shrugged.

"You must be going for the big boss."

"Mr. Brooks?" Her eyes widened. "You have to be kidding. He must be at least fifty."

"But he's rich," Jennifer pointed out.

"Thanks, but I'm not interested."

"Maybe I should be." She smiled, then turned to go back to her work. "Have a good weekend. If you can."

Lexie let out her breath like a sharp breeze across the stack of papers. No way would she get any more work accomplished this late in the day or in the mood she was in. She started to put away her things. Maybe she could tidy up a bit until the clock struck five.

Nicole interrupted her musings. "I see you had a visit from Jen."

Lexie closed her mouth and wished she hadn't confided in Jennifer about Theo.

"What did she want, to catch some of your leftover men? You're breaking a lot of hearts, you know," Nicole persisted.

Lexie glanced at her coworker. "It's nothing to joke about. I just told Darren I have plans for the weekend, and word's spread around the office already. I honestly don't need this drama. I'd simply like to come to the office every day, do my job, and go home."

"Then you'd better find something to make yourself ugly because right now you're like a magnet."

"I wish I could laugh with you. At the rate I'm going, I won't have a male friend in the office."

"At least the women will like you." Nicole watched Darren walk to his desk. "Hmm. Maybe I should find an excuse to go over to his desk and let him cry on my shoulder."

An hour later Lexie arrived at the day-care center in the nick of time. Another minute and she would have been charged an aftercare fee. The daily stress of the thin time margin between her job and day-care location was putting a strain on her. But Piper had already made friends, and the center was on the bus route for Piper's preschool, which helped. Changing seemed to be out of the question.

Tired from a full week, Lexie looked forward to getting home. She took Piper by the hand and was heading out the door when the center's owner stopped her. "Mrs. Zoltan, I need your payment for this month."

This month! Already? Had the time passed by so quickly?

Lexie knew writing a check for the full amount would be foolish, considering the balance in her checkbook. "I'm sorry, but I don't have the money with me today. May I bring it to you next week?"

"Mrs. Zoltan, I've let you slide this long. You must catch up, or I'm afraid—"

"I know. And you're right. I'm sorry. If you can wait until I get paid next week, I'll pay you for this month and the next."

Lexie wished she didn't have to make such a rash promise. Keeping it meant she would have to be late with her electric bill. Yet she had to make sure Piper stayed in a good day-care situation.

"All right. I can live with that."

She took Piper's hand again, drawing her away from another little girl whose mother was sure to be charged a late fee. At least Lexie had been spared that much.

"Mommy," Piper said on their way to the car, "don't we like Theo anymore?"

Lexie was used to Piper's talking about what happened in preschool that day. The question about Theo took her by surprise. A tear formed in her eye. She managed to wipe it away before Piper could notice. Lexie turned her head and pretended to study the summer sky, then hurried Piper into the car, hoping she might forget her question.

"Well? Do we?" Piper persisted.

Lexie started the car. "Of course we do. What makes you ask such a silly thing?"

"We never see him anymore—that's what. He's supposed to help me find more rocks."

"I know, Honey. But Theo is just a friend of ours. He was there for us when we needed him. But now we can't expect him to come over every single day."

"But can't he come over sometimes?"

"Maybe. We'll see."

"That means no."

Lexie was thankful she spotted a fast food restaurant at that moment. She pointed to the colorful sign. "Look. Want a hamburger?"

Piper clapped her hands. "Yay!"

Lexie pulled in to the parking lot, choosing the drive-through so she could take the food home. A glass of water at home was cheaper than a beverage at the restaurant.

As they waited in the long line, Piper hummed a little song to herself. Lexie wiped away another tear and wished she were happy enough to sing.

Why am I so weepy?

She fumbled through the ashtray, which she used to hold her spare change. Enough had accumulated for her to pay for dinner.

Money. Why does everything have to be about money? *Because I don't have enough—that's why.*

She mentally reviewed her financial situation. Social Security checks had been arriving for Piper since Curt's death, but of course they weren't enough to cover their living expenses. The most worrisome at present were mounting credit card bills. She had been putting the minimum toward them each month, which was enough to keep those creditors from calling her at work or at home. But she had failed to pay anything on two other bills the past month. And interest on the debt kept her from making much progress toward paying off the bills.

But how could she ever hope to catch up? Food, rent, and utilities had to come first. Living with Kassia had helped initially, but that could never have been permanent. Not as long as she wanted Piper to be with her.

She took a moment to listen to her daughter's excited voice. So much time had passed since Lexie had been that happy. Not since—

No. She wouldn't think about Theo. He hadn't called since that day at the apartment. By now he had probably forgotten about her. Maybe he was sitting on the beach at that moment. Maybe he'd already met someone else. Maybe they were sharing an umbrella, drinking ice cold drinks, laughing together—

No. I can't think about it. I set him free—practically threw him out on his ear. He has every right to go wherever he wants, to see anybody he wants to see. He deserves better than to be stuck dealing with my problems.

Lexie added the numbers in her head. Even with the new apartment, her salary at work and Piper's checks should have provided enough. They'd never live in luxury on their income, but they should be able to live well enough. With a little bit of money management.

Money management. That was something she had never mastered. Finances had always been tight for Mom and Dad, which meant Lexie knew how to shop for her needs on a slim budget. She had picked up a few tricks by watching them, but she still couldn't understand how Mom managed to turn an old chicken carcass into a delicious soup that could last a week or make a pair of socks last forever. She did remember one big piece of advice. Dad said that a new car smell was the most expensive perfume in the world.

The car payment! How could she have forgotten? The long white envelope was sitting on her desk at home, waiting to be stuffed with the month's check that was due in three days, a week before her next paycheck would arrive.

Maybe she should write the check and "forget" to sign it. Or she could tell the company that the statement got lost in the mail.

Dear Father in heaven, have I become so desperate? I know You'll find a way. I don't have to dishonor You to meet my bills.

"Help!" she whispered.

"What, Mommy?" Piper asked from the backseat.

The child who couldn't hear her mother ask her to pick up her toys could hear a softly spoken prayer.

"Nothing, Honey." She pulled up behind the car in front of her, which had just moved up so Lexie could take her turn at ordering from the menu. She rolled down the window. "One child's meal. Hamburger. That's it."

Lexie hardly felt like eating, so what was the point of ordering anything for herself? Instead she thought about how to solve her car payment problem. She had to keep the car so she could drive to her job. She had to get help from somewhere.

Theo's face flashed through her mind.

No. I won't call him, especially not after the way I've treated him. I'll call Kassia. She's smart. She'll know what to do.

∞

Theo heard his phone ring as he was about to sit in front of the television with a cup of tomato soup. He'd been engaged in mind-numbing paperwork all day at the office and was in no mood to explain to a telemarketer that he didn't need replacement windows, a heating system checkup, or a free trip to some exotic locale just for listening to a brief sales presentation.

He glanced at his watch. Six in the evening. Yep, it had to be a telemarketer. Who else would call at dinner? Theo remained in his chair, turned up the volume on the TV, and swallowed a spoonful of soup.

He listened to the announcement on his answering machine, then heard the beep.

"Theo, if you're there, pick up."

"Kassia?" he exclaimed as if she could hear him. "What are you doing calling me?"

"Okay," Kassia said. "I guess you're not there. Umm... listen, when—"

He scrambled to reach the phone. "Hey, Kassia. I'm here."

"Screening your calls, eh?"

"I thought you were a telemarketer."

"When are you going to join us in the twenty-first century and get caller ID?"

"As if that would help. It would just read 'out of area' for most of those unknown callers, and I'd still be screening my messages."

"Well, you have a point, but it works great the rest of the time."

"Now if you were planning to sell me caller ID or anything else, for that matter, I'd be forced to hang up."

"After I finish, you'll probably wish I were selling vacuum cleaners."

Theo set down his soup, bracing himself for what was certain to be bad news. "What's wrong?"

"It's Lexie."

"Lexie?" His heart seemed to skip a beat. "Is she all right?"

"Yes."

"Oh, no. Something's happened to Piper."

"No, it's nothing like that," Kassia assured him. "Calm down."

His voice turned serious. "How do you expect me to react when you call and act like the world's ended? And if it's not an emergency, why isn't Lexie calling me herself?"

"She's too embarrassed," Kassia said. "She doesn't even know I'm calling you. She'd probably kill me if she knew."

He had a thousand questions, and he wanted answers to them all. "So what's up?"

"It's her car. She's behind on her payments, and now the finance company is threatening to repossess it."

Theo couldn't suppress a laugh. "That pile of junk? I can't believe they'd bother."

"I know. But apparently they are bothering. And they've started calling her at work and at home."

"No wonder she's embarrassed," Theo agreed. "I guessed she wasn't in the best financial shape, but I had no idea things were that bad."

"Neither had I. She called me earlier. I could tell she was crying, but she wouldn't admit it. This is really serious, Theo. If she doesn't have a car, how can she get to work?"

"How long have they given her to pay?"

"I'm not sure."

"Why did she call you? Did she ask for money?" He hoped

Kassia would answer in the affirmative. Theo could lend, or even give, Lexie a few hundred dollars to get her out of such a predicament if necessary.

"She didn't ask, but I offered a couple of hundred dollars. That's all I can spare at the moment. She wouldn't take it," Kassia said. "She only wanted advice."

"What did you tell her?"

"I didn't know what to say. I told her things were bound to get better. As soon as I hung up the phone, I called you."

"I'm glad you did."

"Don't tell her you heard from me, okay?"

Theo wasn't sure how he would manage that, but he'd figure out a way. "Sure. But I'm not sure what you want me to do."

Kassia didn't answer right away. "I don't know. Just check on her, I guess. See how she's doing. Maybe if you do, she'll open up."

"Maybe so." Theo remembered how he had been in prayer for Kassia. "Speaking of opening up, how are things with Brad?"

"What's that supposed to mean?" Kassia's voice was sharp.

"Nothing. I just wondered if you'd like to talk about it."

"There's nothing to talk about," Kassia snapped. "And I'm in no mood for a lecture. I've had plenty of advice from her, thank you very much."

Whatever Lexie said must have hit a nerve with Kassia. Theo decided levity was the only way to go. "Did you ever see the T-shirt slogan that says, 'I yell because I care'? Well, Lexie and I lecture because we care."

"Very funny."

"Throw that stone down, Kassia. Remember—you're the one who called me about Lexie, and you didn't even tell her first."

Kassia groaned. "Why can't I talk to either one of you without feeling thumped by a Bible?"

"Maybe God's trying to tell you something."

"If He is, I'm not sure I like it very much."

"I don't like everything He tells me, either."

"Really?" Kassia sounded surprised. "I can't believe that. Not as devout as you are."

"I can't vouch for what other people have found out, but in my experience the more I sense the Lord's presence with me, the more He seems to communicate with me. Maybe it's just that I can hear Him better."

"That sounds like something you'd say," she answered. "Anyway, if it makes you happy, I'll have you know I'm not seeing Brad."

"That's probably a good thing."

"Whatever. See you later."

Before Theo could respond, Kassia hung up.

Normally he might have called Kassia back and apologized, but Lexie's situation was more urgent at the moment. Theo didn't waste time. He gulped down his soup and decided against the pint of ice cream he'd planned for dessert. Instead he logged on to his computer and stretched his fingers. If knowledge was power, Lexie would be fully armed if he had anything to say about it.

fourteen

Lexie was about to tuck Piper into bed when the doorbell rang. The little girl jumped out of bed and ran to the door, all the while shouting, "We have company! We have company!"

"Shh, Piper," Lexie told her. She wanted to look through the peephole and see who it was before opening the door. Now that Piper had yelled loudly enough for the neighbors in the surrounding apartments to hear, ignoring their caller was no longer an option.

Theo! What's he doing here?

"Who is it, Mommy?" Piper asked.

"You'll see." Lexie turned the deadbolt and opened the door.

Piper gasped. "Theo!"

Without hesitation she ran into his arms. Lexie couldn't believe how natural they seemed together.

Theo nodded at Lexie, then spoke to the child. "Hey, how's my little archaeologist?"

"Arkee—arkee." She wrinkled her nose. "Huh?"

"Archaeologist. They dig in the ground to find neat things like rocks."

"But I find things, and I don't dig in the ground." Her head turned in Lexie's direction. "Can I dig in the ground, Mommy? I'll find lots more rocks then."

Lexie groaned. "I'm sure you will, but you can find plenty of rocks without digging." She smiled and shook her head at Theo. "Did you have to give her more ideas?"

"Sorry." Theo chuckled. "Here's an idea, Piper. Shouldn't you be in bed by now?"

"No! Mommy was gonna read me a story," Piper said. "But

now you can read it with us. Like you did at Grammy's."

Piper had missed Theo as much as she had! If a heart could flip-flop and melt all at once, Lexie's heart did at that moment. "Piper! Just because Theo's here doesn't mean he has to do whatever you want him to."

Theo bowed to Piper as though she were a princess. "If your wish is for me to read a story to you with your mom, then your wish is my command, young lady."

"If you want to do that, you'll have to come in," Lexie said over Piper's laughter. She opened the door wider and watched Theo enter. Her heart betrayed her with its rapid beating. "It's been awhile. Where have you been?"

"Where have I been?" Theo gave her a questioning look, then shrugged before offering an answer. "Work. Home. Same old treadmill."

"Me, too. I'm glad you stopped by," she ventured.

"Really?" His voice was little more than a whisper.

She nodded. "It's nice to have a break."

"Oh."

Seeing his crestfallen expression, Lexie touched the top of his hand for a moment. Her fingertips tingled at the slight contact. "I'm really glad you came by."

"Then so am I."

Lexie made coffee for the two of them, then gave Piper a bedtime snack of milk and an apple. Theo talked about nothing in particular; yet she found his conversation pleasant. As usual they agreed on everything that mattered. Since she'd been working in the office, Lexie realized the rarity of an agreeable friend.

Was his visit a peace offering? Or did he have some other reason for stopping by?

Lexie glanced at her watch. "Well, I can't believe it, but it's after eight." She shook her finger playfully at Piper. "It really is bedtime for you now. Way past your bedtime, in fact."

"Story! Story!" she called out, then dashed into her room.

Lexie stood. If Theo sought a relationship other than friends, she couldn't offer him that. And allowing him to linger after Piper was asleep was too risky—for them both. "Guess I have the rest of the night planned out for me."

"Don't you mean for us?"

"Us?"

He stared at her. "I promised to help read the story, remember? If I don't, she'll never forgive me."

Lexie wished she could think of a good reason to insist he leave, but she couldn't. "True. Piper has a long memory."

"Come on!" Piper shouted from her room. "I picked out a story."

"I hope it's not *Green Eggs and Ham* again," Lexie whispered as they both headed for the little girl's room. "As much as I like Dr. Seuss, I don't think I can take another night of the same thing."

Lexie was relieved to discover Piper had chosen *The Three Little Pigs.*

"But this story doesn't have a princess," Theo teased.

"I know. But I want to see you be the Big Bad Wolf."

"But I want to be the Big Bad Wolf," Lexie complained.

Piper shook her head. "I'll bet you aren't as good as Theo. Isn't the Big Bad Wolf a boy?"

"I suppose," Lexie agreed.

"We don't always have a boy here to be the Big Bad Wolf."

Lexie felt both grief and regret at her daughter's statement, but Piper's little face didn't change expression. Funny how children could say things and not seem to feel the same effects as the adults around them. Lexie supposed such obliviousness was a gift.

Theo and Lexie sat on each side of Piper and put on a show for the delighted little girl. Lexie read the parts of the three little pigs, and Theo gave an enthusiastic portrayal of the Big Bad Wolf. His voice was gruff when he spoke. He inhaled with gusto as he promised to blow down each house.

Despite protests from Piper that they should read another story, Lexie convinced her there was always tomorrow night.

"Time for prayers." Lexie and Piper knelt beside her bed as usual. Lexie realized she might have been shy kneeling in front of anyone else, but she didn't mind Theo's presence. When he joined them, she felt closer to him than ever.

Lord, I wish things were different. I wish I could be the wife Theo needs. But I still wouldn't give up my little girl for anything. Not even Theo.

Lexie only half listened to Piper's familiar recitation thanking God for a long list of friends and family—until she heard Theo's name. Opening her eyes, she glanced at Theo and saw a sad smile on his face.

As they stepped out of the room, Lexie deliberately set a light mood. "Ever thought of going into theater?"

"Only if I can be the Big Bad Wolf," he replied. "Or maybe Prince Charming."

"You'd have no problem with either of those roles." As soon as the words left her lips, Lexie wished she could take them back. She had promised herself she would do nothing to encourage Theo. So why did everything she say seem to contain the underlying message that she wanted to be with him?

She didn't sit down when they reached the living room. Her heart didn't want Theo to leave, but her head overruled. "Well, I have a big day tomorrow, and so do you, I'm sure."

"I guess so. At least it's past Hump Day."

"Hump Day?"

Theo's eyes widened. "You've never heard of Hump Day? It's Wednesday, of course. We've gotten over the hump of the work week."

"Oh. I guess I probably heard that somewhere before. I'd just forgotten." She folded her arms and tried to think of another excuse to urge him to move on, but nothing came to mind. Apparently she was stuck with company for awhile longer. Not that she minded.

"Piper and I made some brownies yesterday. Want one?" she offered.

"Sure—why not?" He plopped down on the sofa as though he belonged. Studying him, she realized he fit well into the picture.

"How about a soda, too?" he asked.

"I don't know. I'm afraid that might not be enough sugar for you." Nevertheless, she headed toward the refrigerator to fulfill his wish.

"I doubt it."

Lexie searched for the last soda she thought she had saved. "Looks like it's milk for you. I ran out of soda. Sorry."

"Is this a conspiracy?"

"Maybe it is." She smiled at him and poured a glass of skim milk instead. "This will go better with a brownie anyway."

He bit into the square. "Mmm. You and Piper make a good team."

"I know. Sometimes I feel as if it's just the two of us against everybody else."

"Against everybody? How can you say that? You have lots of friends and family to support you."

"Emotionally, yes." She crossed her arms over her chest, a gesture she knew looked defensive, but she didn't stop herself. "And financially, too."

"Are you sure about that?"

"So that's what this visit is all about? You're afraid I can't handle the rent on this apartment, and you've come to make sure I'm still living here?" She kept her voice light and teasing, though she knew Theo would see the truth in her words.

"I'm sure you can handle anything. You've done better than I would have in your position, with the move, getting settled in a place you haven't lived in a long time, and now getting Piper settled in."

"It's been a struggle, but we manage."

"Are you sure?"

She set her own brownie on the side table. "Okay. Spill it. What do you know?"

"Is there anything to know?"

Lexie had confided in only one person who knew Theo. "Kassia. You've talked to her, haven't you?"

"What makes you say that?"

"The fact that you answer every question with a question, that's what." She narrowed her lips. "So what did she tell you?"

"Now don't get mad at her. She's just concerned, that's all."

Lexie's stomach suddenly felt like a ball of lead. So Kassia had run to Theo and told him her troubles. "Tell me what she said."

"She just hinted that you're having a little bit of difficulty meeting your bills."

"Well, I have to admit—that's an understatement. I'm not doing too bad, really, except right now I'm worried about the car. I got behind on my payments, and now they want to take it. I'm not too proud to take a bus to work, but having to drop off Piper and pick her up from day care is the problem. I really need a car if I want to function with any efficiency." Lexie realized she was babbling. "But why did Kassia tell you? It's not your problem."

"She thought I could help. And I can. Well, sort of." He lifted his forefinger in a way that reminded her of a teacher. "Did you know that some day-care centers are funded by a charitable organization? Others are subsidized by the government."

Lexie remembered how much money she owed Piper's center. She shuddered at the mess she had made for herself. "I don't guess our center is subsidized. No one said anything."

"Do they know you're a single mother?"

She nodded. "I had to put all the information on the emergency contact form."

"Then they should. Maybe they just didn't pay enough attention to your form. But as far as I know you're eligible to apply for low-cost day-care since you're a single mother," he said. "Who knows? You might even be able to get good care for free."

"Free?" Lexie didn't like the idea of charity, but she was in no position to be picky. "Really? I had no idea. But how did you know?"

"One of our secretaries is a single mother. We took her out to lunch for Secretaries' Day, and she was talking about how she had to get subsidized day care. She said she didn't know how she'd make ends meet without help."

"I'll definitely look into that. Thanks, Theo."

"Problem solved then." A big grin spread across his handsome face.

"I wish! Sure—if I'm able to get help with day-care expenses, that would be great. But that's only part of the picture. I have other bills, and I'm way behind."

"On more than just the car?"

She nodded. "I'm afraid so."

"You're not making the minimum payment each month, are you?"

"I try to pay a little more, but it's hard."

Theo gulped, a gesture that left Lexie embarrassed.

"I don't want to talk about it. Let's change the subject."

"Changing the subject won't make it go away. Let me help you if I can."

"I don't see how you can help any more than you already have." Lexie rose from her seat and took her plate into the kitchen. Their discussion seemed to be degenerating into an argument, something she didn't want to happen. She had argued too often about money with Curt. Why was she repeating the pattern with Theo—even if he was just a friend?

"My dad's a banker, and I learned a lot from him. Maybe I can help you sort things out. For instance, do you buy things on sale?"

Now she had him. Lexie strode toward the couch and sat beside him. "I certainly do. In fact, I buy almost everything on sale. I make sure to use plenty of coupons at the grocery store."

"That's great, but I don't just mean food. I mean clothes and things like that."

"Of course. Why, just this week I bought a new pair of shoes on sale. In fact, it was a sale with an additional 20 percent off." She was certain he would agree she was a smart shopper.

"That's great. But you charged them."

How did he know? "Yes." She almost blurted out that she didn't visit the consignment shop because she didn't have the cash. Perhaps the shoe purchase could have waited; but they were perfect for work and church, and the sale had been too good to resist. "My church shoes have some wear on them, and I have to keep my wardrobe looking halfway decent for work."

"I know. You have to present yourself well if you want to hold an office job," Theo agreed. "But if you buy things on sale and pay the credit card companies interest on what you buy, you're not saving the first cent."

Lexie didn't answer right away. She hadn't thought of it that way. "I guess you have a point."

"I hope you don't mind my saying so, but the first thing you should do is pay off as many of those cards as you can."

"I would if I could."

"You could use your savings. You'd still be ahead on interest, unless you have some kind of deal I don't know about."

"Sorry. My savings are gone."

"You were married awhile. Did you and Curt buy any real

estate, maybe a piece of land in North Carolina you could sell now?"

"If only we had. No, we always rented." The next part was difficult to say, but Lexie had to tell him. "Curt's funeral expenses ate up everything we had accumulated, which wasn't much. I couldn't believe how much everything cost."

"Oh, that explains it then."

Lexie looked at him. "That explains why I seem so irresponsible?"

"You don't seem irresponsible. Who would have thought you'd have to even be thinking about a funeral for your husband at your age?"

Lexie nodded and looked down. She turned away and grabbed a tissue from the box on the side table. Maybe if she wiped her eyes now, she could keep tears from falling and mascara from running.

She was so absorbed in getting the tissue that she didn't realize Theo had moved closer to her. He put his arm around her shoulder. His arm felt warm, protective. Close like that, she could smell his citrus cologne. After all these years he still wore the same scent. Until they had met again, Lexie had forgotten how it smelled on him. But now when she inhaled the pleasant aroma, she felt as though she had arrived at a familiar place. A place she liked.

"I'm sorry. I know it's painful still for you to talk about Curt. And it probably always will be. Especially because of Piper. My heart goes out to both of you." His voice, barely above a whisper, offered comfort.

So he thought of Piper, not just me.

She patted his hand. "Thank you."

He squeezed her shoulders, then moved back until their gazes met. "I have an idea. You say you and Curt never owned a house, right?"

"You say that like it's a good thing."

"It might be," he said eagerly. "All you have to do is exercise a little bit of discipline and pay off your cards, or at least get the balances manageable. Then I can ask my dad about finding a home loan for you. First-time home buyers get a lot of breaks, especially if they don't make much money. You won't be able to buy a mansion, but something reasonable in a good neighborhood will help you in many ways."

Lexie raised her hands. "That sounds great, but hold on. I don't think you understand. I'll never qualify for any kind of loan with my credit as it stands now. Not counting what I owe on my car, I'm more than ten thousand dollars in debt."

"Ten thousand dollars?" Theo's eyes widened, and he took in so much air Lexie thought he might suck all the oxygen out of the room. "You're kidding."

"I wish I were."

She watched as he looked around her apartment. The furniture was a mishmash of castoffs, rentals, and pieces of cheap veneer that Curt had assembled himself. "I know. It's hard to believe I owe so much, isn't it? I sure don't have a thing to show for it. Except a decent burial for Curt."

"I'm sorry. I didn't mean to seem as if I were passing judgment," Theo said. "You've had some tough breaks. I can only imagine what that's been like for you."

"That's okay. I don't expect anyone to understand if they haven't been through it."

"I wish I could write a check for the whole amount and make your money problems disappear like that." He snapped his fingers. "But I can't."

She took his hand in hers and squeezed it gently. "I appreciate that. I really do. But even if you could, I wouldn't accept your money. I don't need a knight in shining armor." Fresh tears betrayed her, flowing down her cheeks. "Theo, I don't know how I'll ever be a good mother to Piper. At least, not the mother she deserves. She deserves a responsible woman, someone who has everything all together. She doesn't need someone who's made such a mess of her life, like me."

"I wouldn't say that."

"Don't try to defend me," she said. "When I first came here, I thought that with the salary I was making I'd be in good shape in less than six months. But I hadn't counted on everything being so expensive or Piper's going to the hospital or our having to move out of Kassia's place so soon. I don't own a thing of value, really. Even the couch you're sitting on is rented."

"That's nothing to be ashamed of."

"I'm not ashamed. It's just that, well, I came here in part because I didn't want to depend on my parents so much. After Curt died, Mom kept Piper for me so I could work. I was living rent free, too. I see now that I didn't know what a good deal I had. I guess I never grew up. I'm beginning to think I never will."

"Yes, you will. You're just finding out—a little late in the game—that the price of independence is high. But maybe it's not as high as you think." He thought for a moment. "What about insurance? Maybe Curt left you some money you don't even know about."

Lexie cried even more at Theo's suggestion. "He didn't have any insurance. There was no money when he died."

"What?" His face was flushed. "How could he have been so irresponsible? He knew he worked in a hazardous field and that you had Piper to take care of!" He let out a sharp breath. "You know something? Since that accident was work-related, the construction company should have offered you a settlement at least. If they didn't, I think you should hire a lawyer first thing tomorrow."

"No, it's not like that at all." She placed her hand on his arm. "Curt's death had nothing to do with the construction company. It was my fault."

"What did you say?"

Lexie swiped at her eyes. She had given up on not smudging her makeup. She could only imagine what she must look like, with brown mascara and gray eye shadow running down her face. "It's true. It's my fault he died. Neither one of us was good at managing money. No matter how much Curt earned, we barely got by. We never could get ahead. We both wanted what was best for Piper, so she could grow up and have a nice childhood. We didn't want her to remember us scrimping on everything and fighting about money—which we did all the time. I even thought if things got better, we might have another baby." She paused. Making such a confession to Theo seemed strange. She almost wished she hadn't.

"That's only natural," he said without rancor in his voice or face. "Everyone wants what's best for their families."

"Well, I went too far. I suggested that Curt start his own business. At first he resisted, but the more we talked about it, the better of an idea it seemed to be. Then, when he started not getting along with his boss, I insisted. At first he was happy being his own boss. But soon we found out owning a business wasn't Easy Street as we'd thought. He freelanced and took whatever jobs he could. He didn't always win the bid for the work, and the paperwork required to put in all those bids consumed a lot of time for nothing. Everything was so insecure. The work wasn't as regular as we'd expected it to be. Then when we got walloped with more taxes than we anticipated, plus insurance bills for our employees, we were in a mess. We were beaten emotionally, physically, and financially."

"The construction industry was booming, though. He couldn't get his old job back?"

"No. He was in competition with them on several small jobs."

"Since he didn't like his boss, they probably wouldn't have taken him back anyway."

"That's what Curt thought," she agreed.

"So you weren't working?"

"I tried to find something, but the salaries I was offered were too low to justify the expense of working. I was too proud to ask Mom to take care of Piper for me. So Curt took a second job with no benefits. The day of the accident Curt was functioning on four hours' sleep. I think if he hadn't worked so hard, he'd be alive today. I wish I hadn't pushed him so much. I wish I hadn't been so greedy." By now her tears had turned to sobs.

"Don't be so hard on yourself. Curt was a grown man, and he made his own decisions to work so much. You didn't force him."

Regret washed over Lexie. Curt would have died a thousand more times if he could have witnessed her spilling every bad thing about their lives to Theo. "I didn't mean to tell you so much. Curt would have a fit if he knew. He always was afraid of you, you know."

"Afraid of me?"

"He thought you were too much competition. I tried to tell him we were just friends."

"Are we? Are we really just friends?" Theo's voice held no expression.

Lexie's heart skipped a beat.

"I think we are more than friends, and I think you believe that, too." He leaned closer to her. "What are you afraid of, Lexie?"

What was she afraid of? So many things.

She drew in a breath. "I won't ruin your life the way I did Curt's. I want you to leave. And don't bother calling. For your sake, please don't call again."

He rose from the couch. Standing tall, he turned toward her and looked her in the eyes. Lexie held her gaze steady. She couldn't falter. Not now.

Please go. Just go!

The words she screamed in her head refused to leave her mouth.

"I know I came here uninvited tonight. I know I'm the one who's been pursuing you. But I don't believe you don't want to see me again."

She stood. "You're wrong. Just plain wrong."

Theo looked into her eyes. "Am I?"

Theo drew her toward him and wrapped her in his arms in one quick motion. Even though his gesture took her by surprise, he was neither forceful nor demanding. Instead his arms around her felt—natural. As natural as Curt's.

No. I can't.

She wanted to voice her protests but couldn't, not with Theo's lips pressing against hers with a fervor she had forgotten could happen between a man and a woman. As her initial resistance gave way, she softened, dissolving into his embrace as though she were destined to be his forever.

She returned the kiss, her lips touching his clean-shaven face and his mouth that was both soft and strong. How long had she been waiting for this moment?

She was about to savor another kiss when, without warning, he pulled back. "I'm sorry."

Sorry? She wasn't sorry.

"I shouldn't have. I—I have to go."

"But—"

Theo shook his head. "I'll talk to you later."

She reached out to grasp his shirtsleeve but missed.

He had moved fast. And now he was gone.

fifteen

The following weekend Theo looked at the telephone for the hundredth time. He was due to arrive at the church clothes closet at noon; he had volunteered to help with it the second Saturday of every month. The time was almost eleven. If he called Lexie now, he might slip in an invitation to dinner.

"No," he muttered. "I can't call her. I already took advantage of her."

The image of their kiss entered his thoughts. He wished Lexie were there, so he could touch her, hold her, as he'd wanted to for so long. He was sorry he had given in to his longing, a longing he had felt ever since seeing her again. Then again he wasn't sorry. For no matter how many times she told him to get out of her life, he would have the memory of her sweet kiss.

"No. I can't think about her."

He looked at the phone one last time. Resisting the urge to call, he shook his head and hurried out the front door, shutting it behind him.

☙

Lexie sat at her kitchen table and stared at the bills that begged for her attention. How would she manage to get by this time? The juggling act was growing harder and harder.

"Here it is, Saturday night, and instead of getting out of the house and having a good time, I'm alone with a mountain of paperwork, wondering how I'll get by," she mumbled.

At times like this she missed Kassia. Her old roommate would have taken her by the arm and insisted they go out for a few minutes—if only to eat a fast food meal. Or they would escape with a rented movie. At a bare minimum Kassia would offer a few moments of adult conversation.

Her gaze rested on the nearby phone. Ever since Theo kissed her, a picture of him was not far from her thoughts. If she harbored any doubts that Theo wanted to be more than friends before, his kiss left no doubt in her mind now. No man had affected her this way since Curt.

Curt. What would he think about Theo? She knew the answer. He would want her to be happy. But did she deserve happiness, after her greed caused his death?

Father in heaven, thank You for forgiving me! But, Lord, can You help me forgive myself?

If only she could take her mind from her unwelcome thoughts. Maybe if she stared at the phone long enough, it would ring. And maybe if she added a wish, the caller would be Theo.

"Yeah. And maybe if I kiss the blarney stone, I'll attract a leprechaun—and if he doesn't trick me instead, he'll show me the pot of gold at the end of the rainbow."

Piper interrupted her musings. "What's a leprechaun?"

"A leprechaun is a—oh, never mind what he is."

"Is there a pot of gold at the end of the rainbow?"

"Only in the minds of those who wish it were so," Lexie told her. "That's just an old legend."

"Can we look for it the next time we see a rainbow?"

Lexie laughed. "The trick is, no one can find the end of a rainbow."

"We can try!" Piper insisted.

"Honey, if you show that much determination in all your efforts, you'll be a great success in life. And you'll also succeed if you get enough sleep. So I want to know why you're up at this time of night. You're supposed to be in bed."

"But I'm thirsty."

"You can drink some water from the cup in the bathroom."

"But I don't want water. I want lemonade."

"It's too late for all that sugar. Go to bed, please."

Piper's mouth formed a pout. "You're always grumpy when you read the mail. I hate the mail."

"Some days I don't like it much, either." She stretched out her arms for a hug. Piper ran into her arms and shared a brief embrace. "Now can I have a glass of lemonade?"

"I'm sorry—but I said no, and I mean it. Now run along to bed as I told you. Mommy's busy."

"Okay."

"Remember—it's 'yes, Ma'am.'"

"Yes, Ma'am." Her shoulders drooped, along with her voice. "Mommy?"

"Yes?"

"I miss Theo. You were happy when he was around."

Piper's observation tugged at Lexie's heart and mind. "I know, Honey."

"Can you invite him over?"

"Maybe sometime. Now go to bed."

Piper nodded and headed back to her room. Lexie wished Piper didn't have to go to bed, even if their conversation centered on lemonade. She returned to the stack of papers.

At least she could claim one small victory. Because she had always been prompt in the past with her car payments, the bank had agreed to wait another month, but that was it. If she didn't come up with the payments this time, she could kiss her old car good-bye.

And then there was the day-care center. She had to bring her payments with that up to date, too. Theo was right. The price of independence was high.

Theo. She wished he hadn't left. In her heart she had wanted him to protest, to insist he'd never leave her side, no matter what. But why should he have stayed? She had been nothing but rude to him, even though he had spent the evening entertaining Piper, then giving her the best advice and help he could to get her out of this mess. Now she didn't even have his friendship. And it was all her fault.

Under normal circumstances she could call Kassia, but she hadn't spoken to her since Theo's visit. Kassia had betrayed her by running to Theo with the whole story. Sure, she thought she was doing Lexie a favor, but she had only made things worse.

Lord, why do I keep creating chaos in my life? I can't keep money in my pocket or friends by my side. Is it my guilt?

The answer came to her.

The guilt is just an excuse. Your false pride is holding you back.

She recalled a verse from Proverbs. *"Pride only breeds quarrels, but wisdom is found in those who take advice."*

The truth of those words struck her.

When she refused to listen to Theo, they argued. And why didn't she want to listen to him? Pride. Her pride didn't want her to admit she was struggling. Theo only wanted to help, and what did she do? Ask him to leave her apartment—the same apartment he had found for her. And what about Kassia? She had shown Lexie nothing but kindness, and what was her reward? To listen to Lexie's judgment of her and then be cut off after she asked Theo to help.

Lexie knew she'd had to tell Kassia how she felt about her behavior with Brad. Even though Kassia promised she hadn't let Brad go too far that night at the apartment, their public display of affection at the restaurant made them seem too close for a couple on their first date. In hindsight Lexie saw she should have been more loving in the way she'd spoken to Kassia. She wished she hadn't let her anger control her. Spiritual pride must have made her arrogant.

Lord, will You help me overcome this pride?

❧

Theo couldn't keep his mind on the article he was trying to

read in *The Richmond Times-Dispatch*. The machinations of the latest events in the Middle East were complicated enough to require his full attention, so he couldn't hope to glean much from the article unless he concentrated.

His gaze drifted from the article to an ad for a diamond ring. He thought of Lexie's left ring finger, now bare. He couldn't help but wonder if she would enjoy wearing a ring with three diamonds, representing the past, present, and future.

He had abandoned Lexie. She was alone now, with no one to help her sort out the mess she had made of her finances.

"Maybe I was a little bossy," he mumbled. "Maybe that's what turned her off."

The phone rang. It was a little after eight. Didn't the sales calls ever end? Or maybe it was his boss, hoping to pile on extra work. Since Theo was single, everyone seemed to assume he had no life outside work and would be glad to devote plenty of unpaid overtime to the job. Well, they were wrong. Dead wrong. In fact, the previous night he'd gone to a movie with a bunch of the guys. And as soon as he arrived home every day, he took a nice, long jog and often lifted weights.

Then again there he was, staring at a newspaper he didn't want to read, refusing to answer the phone to avoid a sales call and watching the neighborhood kids run through his yard. Maybe his coworkers were right. Maybe he didn't have much of a life. At the same time, mothers and grandmothers of grown women looked upon him as a catch. They were always hinting around, wondering if he had a girlfriend. If only they knew. Would they think he was such a great catch if they could have witnessed Lexie asking him to leave her apartment?

His mood now foul, Theo listened to his message play on the machine. The caller hung up without a word.

Must have been a salesperson after all. His mother would never hang up, and neither would his friends. Not even Lexie.

Lexie. Was there ever a second when he didn't think about her?

For one moment he had thought he might have a second chance at a life he could be proud of. A chance to show love to Lexie and to be the father her little girl so desperately needed.

"Looks as if that's not going to happen," he muttered.

The phone rang again. This time he answered, snarling a greeting into the receiver.

"Hi. Did I call at a bad time?"

"Lexie!"

"I can call back later." Her voice was enough to cheer him.

"No," he protested. "That's fine. I'm fine. What's up?"

"Oh, I don't know. What's up with you?"

"Nothing much. Just reading the paper." If Lexie had called for a reason, she was having trouble expressing it. Not that he was showing himself to be a great conversationalist, either.

"Hey, I was thinking—I want you to know I'm sorry about the other night."

Theo let out his breath. "I'm sorry, too."

"You were just trying to help. I see that now. Actually I saw it then, but I guess I was too caught up in pride to listen."

"Don't lay all the blame on yourself. I was being my usual bossy self."

She chuckled. "Well, Boss, would you care to make up over a cup of coffee sometime? I'd invite you out to a café, but I'm afraid I can't afford a sitter for Piper. Wait. Let me rephrase that." She cleared her throat. "In light of my current financial situation and my efforts to strive toward total financial freedom, I am choosing not to afford a sitter at this time."

"You sound as if you're reading a self-help book. I'm impressed."

"I'm not really. It's a compilation of advice from a lot of books I've been reading lately. I developed a list of guidelines for myself. For instance, instead of saying I can't afford something I want, I say I'm choosing not to afford it. That makes me feel less deprived. So far it's helped. But making up the list was a lot more fun than trying to live by my new rules," she added.

"It's only been a week and a half," he pointed out.

A very, very long week and a half. A week and a half without you.
Aloud he added, "You're not giving up already, are you?"

"I'm trying not to get discouraged. I did have one side benefit, though. Instead of buying them over the Internet or in a store, I went to the library to check out the financial books—"

"Good for you!"

"Thanks. Going into a bookstore is trouble for me. I always end up buying far more than I intend."

"Me, too," he admitted. "So what was your side benefit?"

"Piper wasn't interested in visiting the library before, but when we started going I let her check out some books. She can't believe she can borrow all those books. Now she begs to go back."

"That's great! Isn't it funny how situations that upset us so much can end up having a silver lining?"

"Sometimes."

The pensive tone in Lexie's voice took Theo by surprise. What was she thinking?

"So can you come by after work?"

"I wish I could, but I have a church committee meeting. How about after that? It shouldn't run too late."

"Sounds great. Maybe I can fix you a bite to eat?"

"Sure! I never turn down a home cooked meal. Even a sandwich."

❧

The following evening Theo was glad to sit on the couch

with such a beautiful companion. The rusty color of her blouse was a tone he hadn't thought contemporary women would consider fashionable, since it was a throwback to past decades. He'd noticed women favoring rust colored clothing and wondered why they let designers tell them to wear that shade. Yet no one looked as good in the color as Lexie. The blouse, with a pointed collar—another reminder of past fashions—flattered her light skin and captured the reddish highlights in her golden blond hair, swept away from her face to accentuate her fine cheekbones. When she smiled, her perfect teeth and sparkling blue eyes couldn't compete with the obvious inner beauty she held. How did Lexie manage to look so fresh long after the end of a workday?

"I'm glad you called me and not just because that chicken and rice was so good," he said. "I'd been praying you'd call."

"Really?"

"Well, sort of. I asked the Lord to guide us both. I told Him that if you called, I would take it as an indication He wanted me to give you this." He felt suddenly nervous as he withdrew a check from the pocket of his blazer.

Lord, please don't let her think I'm demeaning her in any way or insulting her. Or worse, don't let her think I'm using You for my will.

"What is that?" Her voice held an edge.

He hesitated. "This will help you bring your car payments up to date, if it's not too late."

"No." She looked down at her plate. "I thought we had this discussion."

"We did. And this is not a handout. This is to help you get to work. It's a lot easier than driving you to work myself every day, although not nearly as much fun as being with you." He smiled, and she glanced up in time to see his expression.

"That's true," she agreed.

"I wish I could bring you up to date on all your bills, but I can't."

"And why not?" Her eyes were twinkling.

He handed her the check, but she still hesitated. He set the check on the table. "Please accept this from me."

"I know you're trying to help, but how can I ever be independent if I take your money?"

"I see your point. Look—if it will make you feel better, you can pay me back with interest."

"Great." She rolled her eyes. "Another debt."

"But not one with a due date."

"I don't know. . . ."

"Don't take it for yourself. Take it for Piper. Ask yourself, are you being the best mother you can be if you pass up this chance to stabilize your lives? Everyone needs help getting started in life."

"You don't mind using guilt, do you?"

"If I have to." He smiled.

Lexie placed her fingers on top of the check and slid it toward her. She picked it up, noted the amount, and nodded. "Yes, this is about what it will take to get me caught up."

"So you'll take it then."

She looked into his eyes without flinching. "Only if you promise to work out a repayment schedule and hold me to it."

He had seen that look in her eyes before. No way would she consider any other option. "All right then. I'll give you a schedule in the next few days, and if you can't live with it, we'll try again. But don't put off cashing that check and paying the bank. If you let them repossess the car, you'll be in trouble."

"I know."

"I don't want you to worry. No matter what you say, I consider the loan a gift."

"But why?"

"Remember Luke 6:34? ' "And if you lend to those from whom you expect repayment, what credit is that to you? Even 'sinners' lend to 'sinners,' expecting to be repaid in full".' "

Lexie grinned. "You memorized that verse just for today, didn't you?"

He cleared his throat and smiled. "I prefer to think the Lord led me to memorize that verse for today."

"What about the verse that follows? ' "But love your enemies, do good to them, and lend to them without expecting to get anything back".' "

"All right. You win a gold star."

"Maybe so. But I have a more important question. Am I your enemy?"

He stood up and extended his hand toward her. Despite the puzzled look on her face, she accepted it and stood.

"I think you know the answer to that."

Lexie pushed him away. "If you're talking about what happened the other night—"

"I am. And if you're waiting for me to say I'm sorry I kissed you, don't hold your breath," Theo said. "I'm not sorry."

"You know something? Neither am I." Her eyes were moist.

"I love you," he said. "I always have, and I always will."

She didn't answer with words. Instead she stepped closer to him. He leaned down to kiss her when the noise of little feet scuffling through the hallway interrupted them. Lexie broke away.

Piper peeked in. "Mommy!"

"Piper, I'm wondering why you're up at this hour."

"I want a glass of water."

Lexie glanced at Theo. "This is our routine, I'm afraid. She goes to bed, and then like clockwork she comes back out asking for water."

"I'd say she's normal," Theo observed.

Lexie shook her head and took Piper by the hand. "I'll be right back."

"Aww!" Piper protested. "You're visiting with Theo. Why can't I?"

"Because it's late. Now come along." She threw him a look of apology.

"I'll be back another time," he promised.

Lexie returned a few moments later, looking a bit irritated and frazzled.

"Now where were we?" Theo asked, hoping to lighten her mood.

Instead of returning to his arms, Lexie stood by the couch. "Don't you wonder sometimes how any couple manages to stay alone long enough to have more than one child? As you can see, living with a child means a life full of interruptions."

"And you wouldn't trade it for the world."

"I wouldn't. But then again I'm not writing a book or traveling the world."

"Neither am I."

"But you hope to someday. Admit it."

Theo shrugged.

"Oh, no. Don't tell me you've given up the idea, especially if you say it's for us. That would be worse."

"I'm not so sure."

"Theo, you've always said you never wanted children."

"I did?"

"Yes. Don't you remember? All through college you reminded me time and time again."

"I did?"

"You're starting to sound like a recording."

"Sorry. I don't remember saying those things. But that was a long time ago. We've both changed a lot since then. Surely you won't hold me to things I said when I was twenty."

"But you also said them when I first came back to town. Especially the part about not wanting children. That's why I didn't tell you about Piper right away."

Theo cringed. "If I said that, I'm sorry. I must have sounded incredibly selfish."

"You're not tied down. You have a right to be selfish. In fact, if you don't want children, you certainly shouldn't have them." She looked him in the eyes. "And that's a shame, too. Judging from the way you are with Piper, you'd make a wonderful father."

"Maybe she brings out the best in me. Sort of the way you do. I must have known that back in school. My heart was broken when you married Curt. But you already know that."

"Theo," she answered, her voice soft. "Don't you realize we parted because our dreams were so different? I knew I wanted a family. Curt had four brothers and three sisters. He wanted to carry on that tradition with me."

"You were planning on eight kids?"

Lexie smiled shyly. "I'm not so sure we would have kept going after three or four, but our house would have been full of love and laughter."

"And you thought mine wouldn't." Despite the harshness of his words, Theo's voice was not condemning.

"Oh, I could tell you had—and still have—lots of love in your heart. But the life you wanted was so different. With Curt I knew I'd be a mother. With you I'd be footloose and carefree, available to pick up and go anywhere on a moment's notice. Sort of like the girl I was in school. I guess I thought you wanted to keep me that way."

"Maybe I did."

He remembered the Lexie of so many years ago, when she was a young woman who seemed to have no end to options in life. Even now, after the tragedy of losing her husband and with her financial troubles, Lexie never seemed unhappy, bitter, or cynical. Over the years she had matured from a spindly teenager to a shapely woman. Her youthful face wore no wrinkles but the look of kind wisdom.

"I'm sorry to disappoint you, but that girl is gone now," Lexie told him. "She'll never return, I'm afraid."

"That's okay. I'm not the least bit sorry to see her go," Theo assured her. "Because the woman who replaced her is far more lovely."

Lexie looked at her feet. "I—I don't know what to say, Theo. As much as I love you, I can't tell you I wish things were different with Piper."

"And I wouldn't want you to." Suddenly Theo understood why Lexie was acting so strangely. "Did I hear you say you—you love me?" His voice was so low and soft he barely recognized it himself.

Lexie nodded. "Don't make me say it again. It hurts too much."

Theo rushed over to her and tried to take her in his arms. She twisted herself out of his reach.

"Do you have to make this any harder than it already is? You know it will never work. We've already had this discussion."

"I remember what you call a 'discussion.' You asked me to leave the apartment."

"Only because I had to. I can't marry someone who doesn't want children."

"Lexie, what will it take for you to understand I've moved past that? And that's all because of Piper. You know I was the youngest in my family. I never was around kids very much. I always was the baby myself, so to speak. I always will be, as long as my sisters have anything to say about it."

"So Piper hasn't scared you?"

"Not at all. My mom said children don't make your life

easier. They make it better. Now I finally see what she means." Theo narrowed his mouth. "Until you came back into my life, I was a fairly selfish person. You and Piper have helped me be a little less self-centered and more outwardly focused. At least I hope so."

She hesitated.

"What's wrong?"

"Nothing."

He knew better. "It's Curt, isn't it? You're afraid you're going to hurt him somehow."

She looked up. Her mouth had formed a surprised *O*. "How did you know?"

"It's only natural to have some doubts. But, Lexie, please don't make me compete with a man who's already gone home to the Lord," he said. "Look—I know this sounds like a cliché, and it probably is, but I don't want to replace Curt in either your life or Piper's. I never want to intrude on the place in your hearts you'll always have for Curt."

"Thanks. I needed to hear you say that. And Piper has helped me realize that. She loves you, you know. She always asks about you if we're apart too long."

"Really?"

"Really."

"And you want me to trade all that just so I can travel and write?" he scoffed. "There will always be time for those things."

"How do you know?"

She didn't have to explain to him what she meant. He knew she was remembering Curt.

"I know the Bible says God doesn't promise us tomorrow. And maybe I won't have time to travel and write. But if not, I can accept that outcome as the Lord's will."

"Are you sure you want to get any more involved with my complicated life?"

"I'm positive. I won't abandon you and Piper. Ever."

Lexie looked around the apartment. "So where is your white horse?"

"He's parked outside." This time, when Theo reached for Lexie, she didn't resist.

epilogue

Lexie took in a breath when she and Theo reached the mountain summit on horseback. The view proved to be everything the trail guidebook promised. A cluster of homes below looked smaller than dollhouses from such a high vantage point. She wondered about the people who lived in them and what their lives were like. Autumn leaves were at their peak in color. A brisk breeze wafted through Lexie's hair, reminding her that winter would touch her icy hands upon them in a matter of weeks.

Lexie couldn't remember a time when she felt freer. Lexie's parents were up for a visit and had taken Piper for the day. Over the past year Mom had been somewhat chilly toward Theo, and even now she was still reticent about Lexie's relationship with him. Yet her objections lessened as she saw how well Theo interacted with Piper. Mom never said it, but Lexie suspected she could see the happiness in Lexie's eyes as well. How could she not want what was best for her daughter?

Over time Lexie had begun to chip away at her bills. She wasn't completely out of debt, but because of discipline and getting the subsidy for Piper's day care, she had finally retired the smaller debts on department store credit cards and was making well over the minimum payments on the major credit cards. She had even cleared her debt with Theo.

She had proven to herself she wasn't helpless, that she could survive on her own. As she became more comfortable with this fact, she found she felt more at ease with Theo. She could love him unreservedly, without thinking he felt only compassion and sympathy for her. While she didn't want a man with no compassion, she didn't want Theo's love out of pity, misplaced or not. Now she could look him in the eye, knowing she was responsible, not dependent.

"This view is something, isn't it?" Theo asked.

She was grateful his observation brought her back to the moment, so she could savor the feeling. "Yes. We'll have to bring Piper here sometime."

"Maybe one Saturday this spring," Theo suggested as he dismounted.

"Or maybe sooner." Lexie dismounted also. After riding, her feet felt strange for a moment as they touched the ground. She shook her legs out before taking the few steps that brought her to Theo's side.

"Yep, God did a pretty good job of creating the world," Theo said.

"I'm sure He's happy to hear that from you," Lexie joked.

"Don't kid yourself. He knows I'm more awestruck than I let on. He knows I think He did some of His best work when He made you."

"Thank you, although I'm sure He's made lots of people who look better than I do."

"Name one."

"I'm looking at him."

Theo laughed out loud. "Okay, so He didn't make you perfect. Your eyesight leaves a lot to be desired."

"You know something? I'll bet if you realized how wonderful you look, you never would have seen all the women who wanted to be with you, and you'd never have wasted your time on me. So maybe your eyesight isn't so good, either. And I'm glad." She grinned.

"Well, if neither of us can see well, maybe I should have saved my money and bought a cubic zirconia." He reached into his jeans pocket and drew out a black velvet box.

Lexie gasped but found herself unable to make another sound.

He opened the box and showed her a modest solitaire that sparkled as the rays of the sun hit it. "So did I spend my money wisely?"

"I don't know. Who is it for?"

"Who is it for?"

One of the horses whinnied.

"No, it's not for you, Lancelot," Theo answered as they both laughed. He looked at the craggy ledge. "I'd get down on bended knee, but—"

"That's okay. So what was your question?"

"As if you didn't know. You're really going to make me take this to the nth degree, aren't you?"

"Yes. Yes, I am."

"All right then. Alexandria Marie Downey Zoltan, will you marry me?"

Lexie pulled on her chin as though she were trying to reach a decision. "Theodore Evan Powers, umm, I'll have to think about it."

Theo's face fell.

"Okay, I've thought about it. Yes, I'll marry you!"

"Yes!" Theo pulled her into his arms in a bear grip, though not too strong or hard. He took the ring out of the box and slid it on her finger.

Lexie laughed with happiness at the sight of the diamond sparkling in the sunlight.

He took her face in his hands. When his lips brushed against hers, even such a slight touch sent sparks through her being. Sparks she wanted to feel forever. To show him, she returned his kiss with fervor.

"Let's get married tonight," she muttered.

He drew his face away until their gazes met. "Tonight? But I, Sir Theodore, your knight in shining armor, won't have time to prepare the castle!"

"Knight in shining armor, indeed!"

"You don't believe me?" He tilted his head toward his horse. "Look."

For the first time, she realized Lancelot's coat was solid white.

A Letter To Our Readers

Dear Reader:

In order that we might better contribute to your reading enjoyment, we would appreciate your taking a few minutes to respond to the following questions. We welcome your comments and read each form and letter we receive. When completed, please return to the following:

Fiction Editor
Heartsong Presents
PO Box 719
Uhrichsville, Ohio 44683

1. Did you enjoy reading *More Than Friends* by Tamela Hancock Murray?

❑ Very much! I would like to see more books by this author!

❑ Moderately. I would have enjoyed it more if

_____

_____

_____

2. Are you a member of **Heartsong Presents**? ❑ Yes ❑ No
   If no, where did you purchase this book? _____

_____

3. How would you rate, on a scale from 1 (poor) to 5 (superior), the cover design? _____

4. On a scale from 1 (poor) to 10 (superior), please rate the following elements.

____ Heroine   ____ Plot
____ Hero   ____ Inspirational theme
____ Setting   ____ Secondary characters

5. These characters were special because?_____
_____
_____

6. How has this book inspired your life?_____
_____
_____

7. What settings would you like to see covered in future
   Heartsong Presents books? _____
_____
_____

8. What are some inspirational themes you would like to see
   treated in future books? _____
_____
_____

9. Would you be interested in reading other **Heartsong
   Presents** titles? ❏ Yes ❏ No

10. Please check your age range:
   ❏ Under 18   ❏ 18-24
   ❏ 25-34   ❏ 35-45
   ❏ 46-55   ❏ Over 55

Name _____
Occupation _____
Address _____
City_____ State_____ Zip_____

Chesapeake

4 stories in 1

*T*he Chesapeake region of the mid-nineteenth century holds days tested by sorrow and renewed by hope. Meet four couples about to be faced with their greatest challenges—can they also find their greatest joys?

Author Loree Lough has woven four faith-filled tales of romance that are sure to bring heartwarming satisfaction.

Contemporary, paperback, 464 pages, 5 ³/₁₆"x 8"

❤ ❤ ❤ ❤ ❤ ❤ ❤ ❤ ❤ ❤ ❤ ❤ ❤ ❤ ❤

❤ ❤ ❤ ❤ ❤ ❤ ❤ ❤ ❤ ❤ ❤ ❤ ❤ ❤ ❤

Heartsong

Presents

Great Inspirational Romance at a Great Price!

Heartsong Presents books are inspirational romances in contemporary and historical settings, designed to give you an enjoyable, spirit-lifting reading experience. You can choose wonderfully written titles from some of today's best authors like Hannah Alexander, Andrea Boeshaar, Yvonne Lehman, Tracie Peterson, and many others.

When ordering quantities less than twelve, above titles are $2.97 each.
Not all titles may be available at time of order.